MARIJUANA
GIRL

Nov, 2007

MARIJUANA GIRL

N. R. de Mexico

Including

A Glossary of Jive

RAMBLE HOUSE

ISBN: 1438238800

EAN-13: 9781438238807

Cast of Characters

JOYCE TAYLOR... An attractive high school miss who took the path from drugs to degradation.

FRANK BURDETTE... A newspaper man with a passion for jazz—and marijuana!

JANICE BURDETTE... A wife who could tolerate just so much.

JERRY BEST... Hot trumpet in a cool joint.

GINGER... Jerry's golden girl... A heroine on heroin.

ANTHONY WAYNE THRINE... A high school boy who learned how to be a man.

ROY MALLON... A "pusher" with a heart as big as a goofball.

DON WILSON... A one-man piano section in a three-ring circus.

ERIC TANGER... A gentleman with one eye on Joyce and the other on his wallet.

PRISCILLA TAYLOR... A prissy aunt.

Marijuana Girl
by
N. R. de Mexico

To Yetena—without whose cooperation
I would have been much better off.

N. R. DE MEXICO

Prepuce

I've heard of this legendary book for years and now, thanks to the generosity of Art Scott of Livermore CA, I am finally able to read, edit and thoroughly enjoy the book. And enjoy it I did. But why? How could I enjoy a book written 50 years ago that can have no relevance to today's world?

Well, the main reason I enjoyed the book was that it surprised me. Just about all of the other thirty or forty vintage paperbacks about drugs in the '40s and '50s that I've read adopt the Harry Anslinger line: purveyors are evil; users are doomed; no one in the scene is clean. But *Marijuana Girl,* although it has some of these elements, has a few characters who use marijuana wisely and make it through the book (and beyond, we presume) without suffering the wrath of Gawd or Man. How progressive of N.R. de Mexico!

The book also tackles sex and other social issues without preaching. You won't find *that* in many books published since Ronald Reagan slept in the Oval Office. The book simply describes the path of Joyce Taylor's descent into addiction as a series of logical steps, most of them brought on by need rather than greed. And though we of the 21st century tend to forget it—or deny it—the U.S.A of *Marijuana Girl's* time was full of needy people. The average urban workers of the '50s lived in seedy apartments, not in sprawling suburban homes. The ones with jobs were the lucky ones.

So why is reading about drugs of the '50s so much more enjoyable and satisfying than reading about drugs of today? It's because we *know* there was a general air of naïvete about dope back then and we can forgive our parents and grandparents for their anti-drug attitudes—just as we forgive them for their sexist, racist and homophobic attitudes. It's much harder to forgive the Mrs. Grundys and Harry Anslingers of today because they damn well ought to know better. After all, they've had plenty of chance to smoke some pot and see for themselves that it's probably the most benign—hell, I say beneficial—substance known to man.

But the main charm of the marijuana underworld of 1950 is its "social" atmosphere. In those days there were night clubs where you could go and smoke pot. There were "pot parties" where people would actually socialize with other people smoking. Of course they were illegal and everybody risked going to prison, but at least the night club or home where the party took place was not confiscated by the state.

In this fourth decade of the modern war on marijuana there's still a lot of weed smuggled into the country and there's even more being grown internally. But most smokers tend to light up at home while watching TV or reading and rarely socialize with other smokers. Indeed, even though many of their fellow workers smoke at home, most people who smoke think they're the only ones who do. Thanks to the Nixon-Reagan-Bush policies, you can get away with using marijuana if (1) you're white; and (2) you keep your mouth shut about it.

Do a thought experiment: imagine all of the pot smuggled into and produced in the United States each year. Better yet, look up the DEA estimates of how many millions of pounds that is. Then divide by the number of people in the U.S. of smoking age (10-90). You come to one of two conclusions: (1) either there are just a few million smokers and they're each puffing away about an ounce of weed a day; or (2) there are a lot more than the 20,000,000 people that the government claims regularly use marijuana. One thing for sure—at $150-$300 an ounce there is absolutely *NO* wastage of weed these days. You drop a one-hit pipeful on the carpet—you get down and pick up every little nugget.

So even though a much higher percentage of people smoke today than did in the 1950s, there is much less socializing. No one admits that they smoke. They couldn't; they'd lose their jobs.

That's why it's so much more fun reading about old-time drugs. Back then the argument was that you'd go insane and kill your family, a charmingly laughable proposition. Now the Bushites are claiming that pot smokers are actively supporting terrorists, a tack that convinces 0% of the people it's purportedly aimed at, and only works on anti-smokers, making them even more rabidly fanatical than they were before the "pot equals terrorism" ads.

Let's face it. Drugs are just as beneficial as they ever were, but they're not as much fun. You have to go back to the good ol' days of N.R. de Mexico, Cornell Woolrich ("Marijuana") and David Dodge ("It Ain't Hay") to find enjoyable scare stories about weed.

Ramble House is proud to make this classic of American drug literature available again to modern readers who are tired of the preaching prissiness of the hypocritical media. The book is full of real people, just like you and me, and it shows how we as a society had a chance to develop a benign and rational relationship with dope—but blew it. We let the wrong assholes rule the roost and now we can only puff gently on our 10 o'clock bongs and flip between *South Park* and *The Daily Show,* thinking we're the only ones on our block who are cool.

Sad, really.

Fender Tucker, Publisher

MARIJUANA
GIRL

Part One

THE GRASS

But should I love, get, tell, till I were old
I should not find that hidden mystery
Oh, 'tis imposture all:
And as no chemic yet the Elixir got....

JOHN DONNE

1 ~ Reflection

"Hubba, hubba," the long thin boy with the unruly hair said, as she brushed past him in the high school corridor. He stopped and turned to watch her as she walked, her dark hair falling to her white-sweatered shoulders, her books held in her folded arms so they squared the heavy roundness of her breasts, her wine-red corduroy skirt a little smooth from sitting, clinging to her hips and buttocks, and her crepe-soled shoes whispering on the highly waxed floor. There was something adult, almost regal, in her walk.

Joyce flung back over her shoulder, "Hi, Tony." She was pleasantly aware of him, carrying herself even a trifle more erectly, so that her breasts molded her sweater into sharper relief as she swung sharp left through the door marked DEAN.

The office of the Dean of Paugwasset High School had been an afterthought of the board of education of that suburban Long Island community. It had emerged, during additions to the building, as a vaguely triangular alcove growing off a corridor, in which Dean Iris Shay and her secretary, Miss Ellsworth, occupied cramped space.

Joyce, with experience born of custom, halted at Miss Ellsworth's desk first, waiting politely in front of it as though Dean Shay's desk were not a scant three feet away. The girl was a little frightened, now, but trying hard not to let it show.

Miss Ellsworth, rather young for a school secretary, looked up sympathetically. She tried to smile reassuringly as she said.

"Miss Shay has been expecting you, Joyce?"

Joyce smiled back, somewhat feebly, and stepped the three paces which brought her to the older woman's desk. Miss Shay turned from the ruled-off schedules that lay on the green blotter; her white hair and bleached blue eyes staring through black-rimmed spectacles, lent her a semblance of cold harshness she did not really possess.

"Sit down, *Miss* Taylor," the dean said. Joyce felt the tremor in her stomach increasing. Whether a student were addressed by her first name or as "Miss" was an accurate index of the dean's attitude. She put down her books on a corner of the desk and seated herself in the hard wooden chair beside it, holding herself rigid and erect under the older woman's scrutiny.

After a moment the dean returned to her schedules, calmly adding up a column of figures before saying, "Miss Ellsworth, would you give me Miss Taylor's record, please?"

The old witch; Joyce thought, feeling the fright growing as she sat waiting for whatever was going to happen. Behind her, atop a shelf of books, she heard the cruelly regular ticking of a pendulum clock that had once been presented to Dean Shay and which, Joyce knew from other sessions in this office, bore the inscription: *To Iris Shay, our beloved mentor, from the Class of 1943.* She had an impulse, swiftly crushed, to pick up her books from the desk and throw them recklessly at the clock.

"Now, Miss Taylor," the dean said when Joyce's record card was given her, "I'm sure you know why you're here." Joyce said nothing. "How old are you, Miss Taylor?"

"It's right there on the record card."

The dean grimly compressed her lips. "Ah, yes. Just turned seventeen and you're a senior."

"Can I help it if I'm smart?"

"Miss Taylor," the dean said, controlling herself with an effort, "we have two thousand students in this school. Obviously, it is impossible for us to watch all students all the time. But with a school population of two thousand— of both sexes—it is essential that we maintain some kind of discipline. I'm sure you agree with this, Miss Taylor?"

Joyce vouchsafed a nod.

"Thank you. I had hoped you would." The dean paused and at Miss Ellsworth. "Terry," she said, "would you mind going to Mr. Mercer's office and asking him for—ah—for the freshman class list for nineteen-forty-seven?"

Ellsworth, taking the hint, hastily picked up a newspaper lying on the radiator beside her desk and scuttled through the door, closing it quietly behind her.

"Now, look here, Joyce," Dean Shay said, "I don't want to make this seem like a courtroom, but you're in serious trouble."

"So I gather." The tremor in Joyce's stomach seemed to reach out and seize her knees.

"Here at Paugwasset, we rely on seniors to discipline themselves for violations of the school rules. The honor system, you know," the dean continued sarcastically. "We permit seniors to write their own absence excuses, for example. I'm reminding you of all this because I think you're an exceptionally clever girl—"

"Dean Shay," Joyce said, managing to muster a tone of bored annoyance, "just what is the trouble?"

"Don't act cute with me, young lady," the dean said. "You're not old enough for it and you're not big enough for it. You know what I'm talking about. I've already spoken to your instructors about you . . . That's why you weren't called in yesterday. I wanted a little time to think this over."

"That's not what I mean," Joyce insisted. "I have a right to be accused of something, instead of just having you go at me like this." She could feel a fine edge of hysteria rising within her.

"If you insist," the dean said.

"I do," Joyce said. "I can't think of any school rules that I've broken of which you have any knowledge."

"You show a fine candor, Joyce, and your argument would do you a lot of credit if you happened to be a lawyer. Unfortunately, we are running a school and not a court of higher jurisdiction. Our purpose here is to train people to live in an adult world. We try to teach not just mathematics or history, but a self-discipline which will make our graduates capable of handling themselves in the community. We expect you to conform not just to the school rules, but to the rules of good taste, and that exhibition of yours in the auditorium yesterday was—well, hardly in good taste!"

"Oh." Joyce said, "that."

"Yes, young lady. That! I know you're going to argue this is limply the prudery of an old maid. Well, maybe I am an old maid. But I firmly assure you that there isn't a high school in the country, and probably in the world, which would tolerate having a student get up on the auditorium stage and—ah—begin to—ah—shed garments. Frankly, I think the study class watching your little performance was as much at fault as you were. We've let the seniors use the auditorium for study periods without any teacher being present because we thought we could depend upon seniors to show self-discipline. Evidently we were wrong. If one of the teachers—no, I won't tell you

which one—hadn't just happened to look in unintention-
ally we would never have known what was going on."

Joyce held her rigid posture in the chair. "Don't you
think it would have been fairer," she said, holding on to
herself to keep her voice from breaking, clutching at the
strange, adult dignity the could sometimes keep in time of
stress—"Don't you think it would have been fairer if the
teacher that saw me had kept her mouth shut."

"Truthfully, Joyce, I don't know. I can't tell you what I
would have done myself. I might have done what that
teacher did—it was a man, by the way—or I might have
spoken to you personally. I don't know. But this teacher
went to Mr. Mercer, and spoke to several other teachers.
Naturally, the fact that this is public information leaves
me no alternative . . ."

2 ~ Reaction

Joyce stepped out of the side door of the school into a long narrow yard where two hundred feet of bicycle racks paralleled a cinder sprint track. She stood for a moment on the stone steps, worn by generations of scuffing feet, letting her mind go on by itself. *Joyce, this is a difficult thing to say, but I believe you need psychiatric help. . . Old Iris. A talent for doubtful limericks does not suffice to earn good grades in English.* The witch. *The physical is important, young lady, but not the only thing in life. I can't prevent you from experimentation—I understand most of you girls, nowadays, have your own theories about that kind of thing—but I can prevent you from carrying on inside the school.* Filthy-minded old maid . . .

Then she discovered herself standing still, and set her feet in motion. Ruth Scott was waiting for her at the street gate. Ruth was shaped like the familiar potato sack, and had honey-colored blonde hair and blue eyes constantly wide with shock at ideas too big for her small mind.

"What happened?" Ruth demanded.

"She kicked me out."

"Out of school!"

"That's right."

"Oh, how *could* she?"

"She did."

"What will you tell your aunt?"

"I won't."

"But, Joy, you'll have to."

"Why?"

"Because what will she think when she finds out you're not going to school?"

"She won't."

"How can you keep her from finding out?"

"I'll just leave the house in the morning and come back at night."

"Aren't you afraid of what will happen if she finds out?"

"She won't. That's all."

"But, what happened? What did Dean Shay say?" demanded Ruth.

"She told me they wouldn't even bring a thing like this before the Senior Court, and I'd have to bring my father in before they would let me come back to school. I told

her my family was in Europe, and she said, well, somebody would have to come in to see them. I said I wouldn't
bring anybody in, and old Iris said, I'm really very sorry
to have to tell you this, but I'm afraid you will have to
remain suspended until you bring in either your parents
or your guardian." She mocked the dean's accents.

"Are you going to write your folks?"

"No. I'm going to get a job. The same as I had last
summer, if I can fix it. I'll be a copy-girl on the Daily Courier." Joyce pointed over Ruth's plump shoulder. "Hey,
isn't that Tony's car? Let's get him to take us for a ride!"

Ruth almost ran toward the convertible parked halfway
down the block. But Joyce walked slowly with her odd
adult grace.

"Want to drive us home?" Ruth asked as she reached
the car.

The dark-haired boy in the front seat, slowly disentan-
gled his much involved limbs and straightened himself up
in the seat; looking at Ruth with a steady, appraising
gaze of his brown eyes. "I might," he said. "Where's Joy?"

"She's coming."

"All right. Get in back." He kicked at the door handle
and the door swung open. Ruth scrambled into the rear
seat, and when Joyce reached the car she got in and
seated herself calmly in front, drawing her skirts tight
about her legs.

"Take Ruth home first," she said. "I want to talk to
you."

There was a loose-jointed ease about Anthony Thrine
that lent his every movement a feline flexibility that also
contained something of beauty, and his manner was as
easy as his movements. He had the assurance and poise
of absolute security—his father was the largest stock-
holder in the Farmers and Mechanics Trust company of
Paugwasset. He was not the president of the senior class,
but he could have been. He was not the editor of the student weekly, because he had refused the job as ill-suited
to his indolent nature. His grades were high in the sub-
jects that attracted him, and barely passing in the ones
that didn't. He had been going, in a tentatively steady
way, with Joyce since the beginning of the senior year. He
had not been the first of the student body to get a drivers
license, but he was the first to own his own car.

His driving was faultless—but in the California manner. He started the car with much tossing of road-shoulder gravel, and took the corners of the narrow tree-lined streets in a squeal of tires. He stopped the car in a long slither before Ruth's house and had the door open before the momentum had ceased.

Ruth got out and closed the door behind her, then hung on it for a moment "Joy," she said hesitantly, "hadn't you ought to talk to your aunt?"

"What for? She'll only nag."

"But don't you want to graduate?"

"I don't give a damn," Joyce said. She tossed her hair. "Come on, Tony. Take me out to Chester's. I need a drink."

Chester's was a roadhouse that led a sheltered existence off the main highway about three miles outside of Paugwasset. Its income traced almost exclusively to the fact that the line of demarcation between the ages at which high school students may drink or not drink is un-apparent to the naked eye, so small is the visible difference between seventeen-year-olds and eighteen-year-olds. Once its dance floor had been the rendezvous of the respectable middle-class citizens who directed businesses in New York and lived in Paugwasset—the upper middle class which kept accounts at Tiffany's, cruisers at Man-hasset and lady friends in Greenwich Village.

But somehow this adult trade had waned, to be re-placed with, first, a collegiate set—the sons of the middle-class, down for the summer from Harvard, Yale and Princeton, down from M.I.T. and in from Chicago. By a subtle contamination these had given place to their younger brothers and sisters, the near-collegians, who attended high schools in Paugwasset and Glen Cove and Mineola, until at length weekly or semi-weekly intoxica-tion at Chester's had become as essential to social pres-tige in the senior class as the use of Dad's car on a Satur-day night.

The place boasted a high raftered ceiling, a long, much-mirrored bar. A juke-box stood near a dais which, on Fri-day and Saturday evenings, supported a good hot trio. The upper panes of the windows were of stained glass which, with the ceiling rafters, gave a vaguely cathedralesque atmosphere to the gaudy whole. And, in a way, Chester's *was* a cathedral. It was a religious edifice in which youth might worship, by imitation, the adulthood so soon to come.

Friendly voices greeted Tony and Joyce as they entered. Chester said, "Hiyah, folks. What's your pleasure?" He was too good a businessman to say, "Kids." You saved that for the older generation.

Tom Houlihan raised a languid hand from his rum-and-coke for a gesture of welcome. Harry Reingold said, "How're things?" Sandra Hart winked at Joyce and said, "Chin up, old man." Mickey Kramer, in one of the booths with a boy just a shade too young for her, pointedly disregarded Joyce and nodded brusquely to Tony before turning back to her escort and her Scotch.

Tony pulled out the table so that Joyce could slide into the booth, but himself strode long-legged to the bar. Joyce watched him without really seeing. With her fingernail she gouged shapes into the cork coaster on the table. Old Iris was like her aunt! No attempt to understand the justification that might explain the act. There had been no point, even, in attempting to tell why she had given that silly little exhibition there on the auditorium stage, because old Iris in her prudery would never have been able to understand. Oh, there was a reason—or there had been. A clear, sensible reason. But now, thinking about it, it was also clear that the reason was something old Iris should have understood from talking to Joyce's teachers. Maybe Iris did understand, but just couldn't condone. Because the real reason, and Joyce knew it well enough, was a compulsion for defiance. Just as the biology paper she had written had been a defiance. They had asked for a general study of a disease. Joyce picked venereal infection. All right, so she was a "bad" girl. A defiant girl.

But the injustice in her punishment, she felt, was that defiance was no crime. Why, lots of famous heroes had been—well, just defiant. Even her mother and father, it seemed to Joyce, were pretty defiant when someone was stepping on their toes . . .

She suddenly fell into reverie.

She tried to remember when Mom and Dad had not been off somewhere, and the recollection was reaching for memories of rare days in long years.

Tony came back to the table, slopping daiquiris at every step. He sat down.

"All right, Joy," he took her hand. "Tell me all about it."

"There's nothing to tell," she said. "I just need a drink."

"Quit kidding. Iris had you on the carpet for the strip act, didn't she."

"Um-hunh. She kicked me out."

"She couldn't. All right, they had to do something to you. After all, that was a pretty raw stunt you pulled. It might have been okay at a party, or something, out in the high school auditorium. I mean, that's pretty raw stuff. But she couldn't kick you out just like that. You've only got another month to graduation."

"That's what she did."

"Can't your folks do anything?"

"What do you mean do anything? They don't even know I'm alive."

"Can't you send them a cable or something? Maybe if you radioed them they'd come back. My old man wouldn't let the school get away with anything like that."

"Listen, all my family ever does for me is leave me lying around with whatever relatives they can find who'll take me. It's been going on like that since I was five—ever since Dad got to be president of Intercontinental."

"You don't mean that kind of stuff."

"The hell I don't. Every darned thing in the world comes ahead of me with those two. The year I was five they went to Mexico, As soon as I was old enough they sent me to a private school, and then left me there sum-mers while they went off to Washington or Texas or China or Brazil or almost anywhere I wasn't. First they could leave me with grandpa and grandma, and then, later on after they died, with my aunt. Anyway, they always found some place to leave me where they wouldn't have to be bothered. And even when they were here they never paid any attention to me—unless I did something really wrong. Once I ran away from a school in Boston. That was two years ago, just before I came back to Paugwasset. You can bet they paid attention then, came tearing in from Chicago by plane." Joyce grinned, as though their frenzied arrival made a pleasant memory. "After that, for about a month, I was a real big deal. There was nothing good enough for me—until they forgot, and dumped me on

Aunt Priscilla, who only stays at the house with me because Daddy gives her so much money to do it."

She broke off, shaking her head, so that her hair swung heavily on her shoulders.

"Can I have another, Tony?"

He rose obediently and went to the bar where Chester mixed a second set of daiquiris. She thought, maybe Mom and Daddy would come back if they knew what had happened. But, no. They were in Europe for the summer, and they would, instead, cable Aunt Priscilla to go to the dean and straighten everything out—and Aunt Priscilla would, too, but her nagging would be beyond endurance; she would be reminding Joyce of it every day, needling her, preaching . . .

Tony set the fresh glass before her and squeezed into the booth. Somebody had encouraged the juke-box with nickels, and a sex-in-a-highchair voice was whispering, ". . . Just a little lovin', honey, would do a lot for me . . ."

On the floor Sandy Hart and Harry Reingold, his six feet tremendously mismatched with her five, were dancing with determined irrelevance to the music.

The May afternoon sun had slipped behind a tree, casting a deep shadow on the stained glass windows, and darkening the room to a warm, intimate mood. Joyce's cocktail filled her mouth and throat with a raw distaste, but her body was becoming warm, and the tense feeling in her abdomen was subsiding and Tony was so good and sweet and wonderful, listening like this to her.

"I thought I would go down to the Courier and get the job this summer," she said, "and then if I'm working they can't say I'm no good, can they?"

"Who?" Tony wanted to know.

"Anybody. Daddy or Mom. Aunt Priscilla or dirty old Iris."

"Whoever said you were no good?"

"Everybody. They all do. You will, too, after a while."

"Why should I, Joy?"

She was a little drunk, now. She knew it. She could feel it. And it was such a wonderful feeling. "Because I'm bad. Because I do crazy things just to get into trouble. Because I got up there and started taking off my clothes in front of everybody. Tony, am I pretty?"

"Of course, honeybun."

"That's the first time. The very first time."

"The first time you—uh—took things off?"

"No. I don't mean that. I mean it's the first time you ever called me honeybun. Tony, you're very sweet to me." She could feel tears of earnestness coming into her eyes. "That's the first time *anybody* called me honeybun— except once Daddy did, after they found me when I ran away."

Just a little self-consciously, because he too was feeling the warm, singing flow of the liquor, Tony put his arm around Joyce's shoulder and drew her close to him, "You'll always be a honeybun to me."

He bent closer and kissed her cheek. She let her head fall back on his shoulder, and her face looked up at his. Her lips were a little slack, slightly parted and moist and glistening. Her eyes sparkled. He bent and kissed her wet lips, letting his tongue caress the pink flesh.

Suddenly he pulled free, a little frightened at the ardor with which her lips answered his. "Let's have another drink," he said.

"Not now, darling. Kiss me again."

"First another drink," Very firm and adult, though his heart was pounding and his breathing seemed to swell him to the bursting point.

Joyce watched him crossing the floor, aware of his tension as of her own. Something inside her kept saying, honeybun, honeybun, honeybun, over and over, as though it were especially important, and she had a confused recollection of her father, holding her close in his arms as he had after they had found her when she ran away, and saying to her, "Poor little honeybun. Poor little baby."

Honeybun. There was a song like that. *Having too much fun—with honeybun*. What's Tony doing with that drink? What's that drink doing with me? Me baby honeybun, Daddy's gone away for fun . . . No. My baby bunting, Tony's gone a-hunting. Gone to get a glass of gin to dip his baby bunting in . . . What kind of nonsense? Pull yourself together, Joyce—you're a big girl now and Tony loves you and you don't need your Daddy . . .

Tony was coming across the floor now, unsteadily attempting to keep the daiquiris intact in their glasses.

Joyce slid out of the booth. Got to help Tony carry the glasses to dip his baby bunting . . . What's wrong with the darned feet? Silly feet, dopey little feet.

Funny about feet, funny about bunny, funny about Tony. Everything was suddenly very funny. Tony and his glasses. Iris Shay and her spectacles. Men seldom made passes at Iris Shay. But they would make passes at Joyce, because men loved Joyce. Funny—ha-ha. Tony had reached the table and was carefully sliding the glasses across.

"Tony," Joyce said, standing there trying to control her feet. "Tony," she said urgently.

"What's the trouble, honeybun?"

"That's it. That's what I wanted you to say. You love your honeybun?"

"I think so," Tony said. "But you'll have to wait till I sit down. I'm concentrating on these daiquiris."

"Never mind. That's all I wanted to hear." She pulled herself very erect, and with a supreme effort seized herself by the arm and escorted herself back to the table. "Let's drink a toast."

"What kind of toast?" Tony had a sudden, somewhat owlish dignity.

"A toast to Tony and his honeybun."

"I dig that," Tony said, "Here's to honeybun." They drank quickly, and the flavor of the liquor was suddenly mild, going down almost like water.

"Don't you think we ought to have another?" Tony inquired.

"I kind of think you've had enough," a voice said, and they looked up to find Chester standing over the table. "Maybe it would be better if the next couple drinks were coffee? Hunh, folks?"

"Were we getting noisy?" Tony asked, very innocently.

"Well, just a mite," Chester said. "Let's put it like this. You're not as lit as you think you are, but you're a little more lit than you ought to be."

"Thank you, Chester," Joyce said, graciously, struggling to slip out of the booth again. "We knew we could depend upon you to keep an eye on us."

"Anytime at all, Joyce," Chester said, "You and Tony are two of my favorite people. And Tony has to drive you back to town. I like my favorite people to get back okay."

"Check," Tony said. He took Joyce's arm. "Well, s'long Chester. Be seein' you."

There was a little difficulty getting the car turned around, but, once on the road, Tony found the machine amazingly responsive to his slightest whim.

The late afternoon sun was warm on their flushed faces, and the wind caught at Joyce's dark hair. She moved closer to Tony on the seat of the convertible, ducking her head to slip it under his right arm.

"Tony?"

"Yes, baby?"

"You love your honeybun?"

"Yup. Intensely."

"Then kiss me."

"Not while I'm driving."

"Then stop driving."

A side road turned off at right-angles to the dirt thoroughfare over which the convertible was bumping. Tony swung the car into it. Suddenly they were in deep woods. The waning sun cast a golden light on the pale spring greens of the trees, and a swift brook gurgled over its stony bed beside the road. Tony halted the car.

Joyce said, "I feel so free and light." She got out of the car and ran to the little brook. In a moment Tony came and stood beside her, putting his arm about her. She turned to him, suddenly and pressed her lips up to his.

Tony," she said. "Let's go wading."

"Okay," Quickly he slipped his sleeveless sweater over his bend, and quickly shed his shoes and socks, rolled up his trousers. Joyce's shoes and stockings fell at her feet. For a moment she stood there, a strange golden-haired wood nymph in a white sweater and red corduroy skirt.

He came close to her. Then suddenly, his arms went about her, crushing her against him, crushing her lips to his lips.

Then she pulled her mouth free. "Honey," she said hoarsely, her voice urgent and almost fierce.

"Not here," Tony said. "Not now."

"Why, Tony?"

3 ~ Shock

Anthony Wayne Thrine, registered owner of New York State motor vehicle number 6N83-215, director under trusteeship of the Farmers and Mechanics Trust of Paugwasset, beneficiary of Freedom Mutual Life Insurance policy number L-615357-M and insured under policy number L-615369-V, former Eagle Scout (annual membership card now four months expired), retired president of the Paugwasset High School Dramatic Society and Senior in the student body of that academy of secondary education, was a seriously upset eighteen-year-old. A morbid fear had been growing in him for hours, and now had reached a pitch where even that source of interminable wonder, the easy, flowing motion of his car, had lost its joy.

He had been unable to reach Joyce all day, though he had telephoned her aunt right after classes, and repeatedly during the afternoon. He had called Ruth too and she had, with her passion for vicarious excitement, immediately begun to worry at fever pitch.

It was almost seven now, and he had called the Taylor house again only a few minutes before. Still no word of Joyce.

He swung his car into the gravel turnaround his father had had installed in the back yard and leaped over the door without bothering to open it—simply because leaping over the door was more difficult than the more ordinary procedure. He was close to the steps of the back porch when a voice caught him in mid-stride. "Tony!" It was his mother. "Tony, you just put that car right in the garage. Don't you dare leave it there in the driveway."

He stopped and called upward to a window. "I'm going to use it right after dinner, Mom."

"I said put that car away."

"Oh, all right. Did Joyce call me?"

Satisfied, the maternal voice lost its shrill pitch, and floated down sympathetically in the suburban quiet. "No. Nobody called."

Unhappily, Tony backed the convertible into the garage and went into the house. The cook, who was also the laundress, said, "Better get washed up, Tony." He didn't answer her, but climbed the back stairs to his father's room, where he used the bedside telephone to call Joyce's aunt.

"Has Joyce come in yet . . . Yes, it's me again . . . No, I just wanted to know if you'd heard from her . . . Well, we had a sort of date after school . . . Is she supposed to come home for dinner? . . . Well, I'm home now, so if you do hear from her could you ask her to call me . . . Thank you . . . Goodbye."

He got undressed for his shower, thinking about Joyce; about her slender body, about the soft smoothness of her lips. He found himself naked, staring at the cluttered top of his dresser. It was a strange litter—a photo of his and Joyce's heads, slightly out of focus; a pocket game the object of which was to guide four little balls into a central aperture; a left-over radio tube from the last repair job on his portable; a pair of broken pliers; a silver-backed military brush set, deeply scored with the initials he had himself imposed with a nailfile; an ink bottle; a locket that belonged to Joyce; a pair of cheap binoculars; an ink-stained doily; a retired hunting knife; miscellaneous phonograph needles; a solid geometry textbook; a cartoon book picked up on the expedition he and Joyce had made to the burlesque show in Union City, New Jersey, which had strangely provided the basis for Joyce's expulsion from Paugwasset High; a key-ring with numerous unidentifiable keys and, finally, a button-covered beanie left over from some remote era like an archaeological relic of a forgotten civilization.

He raced through his shower, dressed quickly and came down to find his parents already seated at the table.

"You're a little late this evening, Tony," John Thrine said, mildly critical. He personally made a fetish of promptitude.

"I was trying to hunt down Joyce Taylor." Tony tried unsuccessfully to smile. "She was supposed to meet me this afternoon." He set about his soup with great protective vigor. What was the matter with Joyce? Where was she? What was she doing? Didn't she know he'd be worried about her? She had been terribly silent on the ride home, last night . . .

It hadn't been very good. None of it had been good. You had both been frightened and unsure and worried, and Joy had screamed that once, and then, after you'd stopped in front of the house, she'd talked about her father—in a way that didn't quite make sense, talking as though her father were to blame for her being kicked out of school.

Tony couldn't figure that part out. After all, she was the one who had got up from her seat in the auditorium and gone up on the stage. Of course, there had been some kidding and horseplay going on before that, but nobody had thought anything about it when she'd got up. And then, suddenly, there she was on the stage, walking back and forth in long strides that stretched out the flare of her light dress, and everybody was watching her. After a moment or so, she had caught the mood perfectly— exactly like the girls in that burlesque show in Union City.

Suddenly she had deftly done something with a zipper, so that with each stride one slim, nylon-clad leg poked into view almost to the thigh. Then, faster and faster, she had whirled in a wild dance.

He remembered how the infection had suddenly caught up the other kids. How they had applauded and whistled, stamping feet to give her a throbbing rhythm for her dancing. Then she had begun a mock "grind", weaving and contorting her body! No one had seen the teacher watching from the back of the auditorium. The whole huge auditorium rang with yelling.

Then unexpectedly Harry Reingold was up on the platform calling, "Come on kids, break it up. You want old pussyfoot in here? Come on, break it up!" And Ruth Scott, tubby little Ruth, was pulling Joyce offstage. Then, as silence descended once more, and the students went back to their books, you had caught a sound from the rear of the auditorium and turned to see a door swinging closed. And you had known, then, that Joyce was in for it . . .

"Tony! What on earth is the matter with you?" Tony looked up at his mother. "What ails you, Tony?" His father put in. "Have you been drinking?"

"I just don't feel so good. I don't think I want anything to eat now. Excuse me, Mom? Dad?" He deserted the table and went into the living room, where he tossed himself upon the couch. This hadn't been the way he'd expected it to happen at all. He had always thought that the first time—well, there would be an exaltation, as well as a tremendous feeling of having achieved adulthood. And it wasn't like that. Not a bit like that. Instead he was terrified, feeling as guilty as though he had stolen money. He was frightened because Joyce had not called, because he had not been able to find her. Supposing she had—well, maybe not that. But you never knew. She had been a little drunk yesterday, and now perhaps she regretted so much that she had been driven to . . . to what? How could you think like that? But after all, wasn't Joyce different? Didn't she have those funny moods, where she did odd defiant things. And if Joy had . . . done something like that, it would be his fault, because he, Tony Thrine, should have had more self-control!

He remembered his father saying: "Tony, the most important thing you must learn in the process of growing up is to exercise self-control." How long ago had the old man said that? A year? Two years? Anyway, it didn't matter, because when the time came that was just what he hadn't done. And now Joyce? What had happened to her? What would happen? Would she—uh—become interested in other boys? Rumor suggested that this was inevitable. But he didn't want her to. He wanted her for himself. She belonged to him. She was his girl . . .

The telephone rang, faintly, as though troubled with timidity. He leaped up from the couch and started toward it, calling, "I'll get it, Dad."

He snatched the instrument from the hall stand. "Hello?"

"Tony?"

"Joyce? I've been going out of my mind. What happened to you?"

"Oh, don't be like that, Tony."

"I've been calling and calling your aunt!"

"How could you be so stupid? I told you not to call there. Do you want her to find out about me?"

All the pent-up worry and fear in his mind turned to anger. "You promised to meet me right after classes. I waited over an hour for you."

"Maybe I didn't feel like meeting you. Maybe I had something more important to do."

"More important! Listen to me, damn you. After last night . . ."

"Last night," her voice was cold, "doesn't mean you own me. I had things to do today, and I couldn't spend the afternoon thinking about some silly boy . . ."

"Joyce," he said, filled with a cold rage, "do me a favor. Drop dead!" He slammed the receiver into place and started back to the living room.

Then, suddenly frightened by his own anger, his own presumption, he ran back to the phone and hastily dialed Joyce's number. Her aunt picked up the phone. "Hello?"

"Hello, this is Tony. Let me speak to Joyce, please?"

"Tony? She's not here. She just called and said she wouldn't be home for dinner; that she was meeting you."

"Did she say where she was calling from?"

"No. Is something the matter?"

"No. Nothing." He started to put the telephone down, then raised it again. "I just got something mixed up. Thanks very much." He hung up. For a long moment he stood there, hating himself for his stupidity, for his meaningless anger. But she must be downtown somewhere. Maybe he could find her. He went to the doorway of the dining room. His father and mother were still sitting at the table. The crystal chandelier over the table cast little glints of light on their faces.

"I'm going out," he said. "Maybe to a movie or something." He went through the butler's pantry and the kitchen and out to the garage, started his car and was passing into the driveway when he heard the telephone ringing again.

He stopped, got out of the car and ran into the house, reaching the hallway just in time to hear his mother say, "No, Joyce. He just said he was going out and he just went out the driveway this minute . . . Wait, here he is now. Joyce? Joyce? Oh . . ." She put the receiver in its cradle, and turned to Tony. "You just missed her. She hung up."

He went back out to his car, got in, and drove through the elm-shadowed streets in the gathering dusk. There was a great lump of self-pity in his throat. It was mixed with anger at himself, at Joyce, at his mother—meaningless anger at them—and a very reasonable anger at the sequence of events.

He drove down Howard Street, braking sharply at the traffic lights, and racing the engine to leap forward as they changed. She must be somewhere downtown. Everything was on Front Street—everything and everybody.

He turned at the corner of Howard and Front. The traffic was heavy. It was Friday evening and the shops were open and people were downtown for the movies. He had to wheel slowly through the jam. Just as he reached Park Avenue, he saw Joyce standing on the curb about to cross. Her slender figure drew his eye like a magnet, and be felt a wave of affection for her. He called to her—though he was on the other side of the street. "Joy! Joy!" She turned, looking about without spotting him. Then she said something to the man standing beside her. He nodded his head and smiled. Together they started across the street, the man—an older man—taking her arm.

"Joy!" Tony screamed again, but the wild honking of blocked cars behind him drowned his voice. Desperately he tried to pull the car close to the curb and get out, but a traffic policeman blew his whistle and the cars behind him honked louder.

He started up, perforce, and drove down the block, at last finding an opening in which he parked. Then he ran along Front Street, panting with anger and disappointment and jealousy. Hs ran all the way along Front as far as Howard, but there was no sign of Joyce.

4 ~ Frustration

For long moments after Tony had slammed the receiver on the hook, Joyce stood with the earpiece still dangling from her hand. It had been so important to tell him, so necessary, so vital to share her good news with someone who loved her. It would have been like going to her father—who was not around to be gone to, who was never around to be gone to. She replaced the telephone instrument. She felt unduly disturbed without knowing exactly why. Yet she had some inkling of it; knew she was terribly frustrated at not having reached Tony, talked to him, rejoiced at the news with him.

The whole purpose of getting the job was defeated. What did it mean if there was no one to understand its importance, no one to take pride in her? But Tony hadn't even allowed her to tell him the good news, hadn't even allowed her to say there was good news. He acted as though he owned her—as though she must always do his bidding, and if he told her to meet him after school then that was what she had to do—and what right had he to demand that?

And then she thought: But I did promise to meet him, and he does love me. Doesn't he? He's supposed to love me. That's what giving yourself to a man means, isn't it? When you sleep with him you love him, don't you? And that makes him love you, too? Doesn't it?

There had to be someone to love you—really love you, want you, possess you, the way your parents were supposed to. And sex was just love, wasn't it? It was love carried to the nth degree. Then she thought about last night, trying to understand herself, trying to get some kind of grip on the fleeting impressions which had shot through her mind, leaving quickly fading traces like fast-falling stars. She thought about the strength with which Tony had carried her to the car, the tenderness of his embrace yet the impassioned need implicit in it—a need no less urgent than her own—the terrible, terrible need to be cherished, to be protected within a warm shield of affection.

You couldn't let Tony misunderstand about this afternoon. You had to put him straight, and then he would come and hold you in his arms and understand and kiss you and tell you how wonderful you were.

She pressed down on the hook of the phone, heard the coin collected, inserted another and dialed Tony's number. There was a busy signal.

She tried again a moment later. Still busy. Now the importance of reaching Tony had assumed the dimensions of panic. She had to reach him. Had to. She tried her own number. "Hello, Aunt Priscilla? . . . Has Tony called? . . . Just now . . . I'll be home later . . . Bye." Then, feverishly, she dialed Tony's.

"No, Joyce. He was here for a while, but said he was going out. He left just this minute."

Joyce said, "Thanks," and let the receiver fall on the hook. He hadn't waited, hadn't wanted her enough to wait for her to call him back. She couldn't hold anyone. Not her parents, who didn't care enough about her to stay with her or take her along with them. Not Tony. Not anyone. Everything was such a mess. Anybody had to be important to somebody. Anybody was worth *something.*

She opened the door of the booth, feeling the tears welling up in her eyes, and tense agony in her knees and stomach. She had counted so much on Tony's love, on giving herself as the means for assuring love.

She realized, then, that she hadn't eaten since morning. Getting the job on the Courier had been so exciting, and the instructions for working so wonderful, and the immediacy of obtaining the job so surprising that the idea of food had vanished entirely from her mind.

She went to the lunch counter across from the telephone booth end ordered a sandwich and milk.

She was trying to reconcile her vast appetite with her emotional anguish when a voice beside her said, "Joyce?"

She swung around on her stool. "Oh, hello, Mr. Burdette. Gee, I didn't expect to see any more of you today."

Burdette was the city editor of the Courier. He was young—thirty-one—for the job, since most of the men over whom he held dominion were his seniors. But the staff was a homegrown product Burdette had been lured from the hustle and bustle of a huge Manhattan daily by an advertisement in Printer's Ink that promised "fine future and rapid advancement to the right man." Moreover the canyons of concrete and the dying lawns of Central Park had never satisfied an earthy passion within him that cried out for greenery and small homes and suburbia.

He had brought with him to Paugwasset his wife, a small son, a passion for jazz amounting to a religion (which he kept reverently concealed from Vail Erwin, his managing editor and immediate supervisor, who believed there should be no religions before the First Church of Christ Scientist). He had also brought an automobile which would have been legally outlawed fifty miles to the west where Jersey state laws protect the citizens from mayhem on the highway and, finally, he also brought the cult of the weed—marijuana.

He was conscious of no wrongdoing in indulging himself in a smoke now and then, though in Paugwasset he kept its use secret from everyone but Janice, his understanding wife. She knew that it was an almost inescapable part of his background, a product of formative years spent largely in the company of musicians, entertainers and others who took "tea" smoking as much for granted as others take tobacco smoking. She knew also that Frank took pride in the fact that he could take the stuff or leave it alone, deliberately resorting to it on occasion for the pleasure it gave him, rather than smoking it willy-nilly by virtue of habit or addiction.

Certainly it did not interfere with Frank's home or his life. But sometimes, as now, he found himself lonely for the highways and byways of New York. As he often pointed out to Janice, whom he had married some years ago in a sudden fit of domesticity, suburbia was fine for commuters who could leave it every morning and return every evening, but it was damned dull if you had to stay there all day long. His heart was in Harlem, and Jimmy Ryan's, and Nick's, and Eddie Condon's. His heart was on Fifty-second Street where small bands and trios and quintets were writing history in marijuana smoke and music. His heart was in these places—and Janice at the moment was away for a week before going to Maine for the summer, where she would take Frank, Jr. to be admired by his maternal grandparents.

This was an annual event, and one to which Frank Burdette could never fully accustom himself. There was something unsound about the idea that toward the end of

May, as spring was turning to full summer, his wife packed up herself and her off-spring and went away for three months. As the summer grew and reached its full height he had always, so far, managed to become adjusted to the idea, and even to enjoy it. Nothing, for example, compelled him to sleep at home of nights—or to spend his evenings alone, for that matter. But the first week or so of this annual departure, which reminded him of salmon heading for their spawning grounds, left him with a feeling of tremendous loneliness.

He had been headed, this particular evening, for a quick snack in the Cozy Luncheonette at the corner of Front and Park. Afterward he would reach a decision: whether to go home and read, go to a movie, or drive into Jamaica and take the subway to Manhattan where something was bound to turn up.

It was in the midst of this storm of indecision, this triple-horned dilemma that he saw Joyce.

He said, "How do you like being back on the job this year?"

"Very much," Joyce said. Her face was grave and serious, but registered pleasure, too. Yet, there was a faint redness around her dark eyes and Burdette decided she had been crying. "It's different from last year, though, now that Mr. Harrigan is gone. He was so nice—"

"Well, I'm not exactly Harrigan, but I hope well get along well."

"Oh, we will, Mr. Burdette. I'm sure we will,"

"Are you going to stay with us this time, or are you going back to school next year?"

"I'm through with school now, Mr. Burdette."

"Look, honey," Frank said, "Don't call me Mister. I'm not that old. My name is Frank."

Joyce blushed. "All right, Frank."

"I thought you lived in town. How come you're eating down here?"

"No special reason. I just didn't feel like going home."

"Meeting your boyfriend?"

For a moment that bothered Joyce. What had happened to Tony? Then she said, "No. I hadn't really made up my mind what I would do."

"Let's move over to a table, shall we?"

"Why not?"

She fascinated him. Frank kept trying to remember that this was only a high school kid—or anyway, just finished with high school. But she was beautiful, and it would have been impossible for him to tell her age. Her dark eyes were steady and wise-seeming. Her hair was a little long for the current fashion, and suggested the softness of immaturity, but her dress—a sleeveless brown shantung with a deep V neckline that bared the first swelling roundness of her breasts, and smoothly shaped her body down to the longish, full skirt—was conservative enough for the most adult tastes. He was not the sort of man who referred to attractive girls as "a dish," but if he had been he would have.

Frank had a theory that all girls are beautiful, provided they're young enough. But he had to admit that Joyce had peculiar individuality in her good looks, rendering her unique, putting her in a class by herself. He had trouble keeping himself from staring. After a while, feeling around for a conversational base, he found jazz. There were names to talk about in common, though she had never met the names, never seen them, knew them only from records. There were Art Hodes, Max Kaminsky, Peanuts Hucko, Bud Freeman, Sol Yaged, and the older names, more magical through tradition, Muggsy Spanier, Louis Prima, the old Goodman group, Jimmie Lunceford—names to conjure with; And there were names to be sneered at— names like George Shearing and Nat Cole, deserters from the higher art; names that were too esoteric, names that had deserted the old tradition of fine jazz for music that was beyond them both, names like Gillespie, Parker.

He learned, to his inutterable surprise, that there was a hotbed of Dixieland growing on a sideroad, and the hot-bed was called Chester's. She offered to go there with him sometime.

He said, "What about tonight?"

She thought of Tony. Could Tony be there? Now, at this very hour?

He went on, "We can drop by my house and pick up the car and drive out—unless you have something else planned."

And she thought of the triumph of meeting Tony, after his rejection of her, meeting him with an adult and snub-bing him. And that would have been all right, but there was something wrong with taking Mr. Burdette—Frank—into a group of kids, something mismatched about it, something that would have detracted from the adult role she meant to play.

"No," she said. "I didn't have any plans, but I'd just as soon not go out to Chester's tonight. Can't we make it another time?"

"Of course," Frank said, wondering why he had asked her in the first place. After all, attractive or not, she was just a kid. And it had been a mistake to ask her to go anywhere with him. Supposing they should be seen? After all, it was a small town, and he was a married man, and this girl, how old could she be? Seventeen? Eighteen? Nineteen? Anyway, just a kid. And he was the respectable city editor of the local newspaper, circulation 13,570. City editors just didn't go out with copy girls!

They finished eating and somehow, mixed in with everything else, he managed to ask her, "How old are you, Joyce?"

"Nineteen." She was proud of the speed of her response.

Then, without meaning to, he found himself inviting her to come into New York with him to visit a very special little haunt of his. A Greenwich Village night club, where he knew all the musicians and they were doing something special with Dixieland—not like bop—but adding to it without destroying it.

And Joyce said, "Gee, that sounds nice. I'll 'phone my aunt and tell her I won't be back until late." She got up and went to the booth,

He watched her as she walked, seeing the slender body, the easy grace of movement, and telling himself, after all, women are supposed to be more mature than men. You don't think of a nineteen-year-old as a kid. Not a girl. Even the state laws recognized that an eighteen-year-old girl could marry without consent.

He watched her in the telephone booth. She was poised and assured as she talked into the 'phone—not like someone asking permission to go somewhere, but someone saying, "I'll be home a little late. Don't wait up for me."

And he thought—dammit, I'm making a fool of myself. But when she came back to the table, smiling and pleased with herself, he suddenly didn't care.

5 ~ Intoxication

The name of the night club known as The Golden Horn was not a reference to the oriental pleasures of Byzantium in the Near East, but bespoke instead the brazen blare of the hot trumpet. Left over from an era when Greenwich Village was still a sinkhole of prohibition iniquity, it had none of the gaudy trimmings of the more modern night spots on Eighth Street. But its dance floor was equally microscopic, its lighting equally concealed.

The chairs and tables ran fanwise in a semi-circle from a small dais and gave an uninterrupted view of six sweating colored musicians. There were no fairies, few intoxicated tourists, and little conversation.

The Golden Horn was a serious establishment, without funny business or sidelines. People who came to the Horn came to drink and listen to the jazz when it was hot.

The air-conditioning was insufficient, the seats wire-backed and hard to the touch of spine or buttock. But the music was the best. Here, from time to time, came Sidney Bechet, Louis Armstrong and other greats of native American music. Here had played such supermen as the immortal Bix Beiderbecke. Here was the temple of a noble art.

Here they came to attend to the important business of drinking, smoking and listening to music.

In taxis and afoot, by bus, subway and private car, they came to have their pulses speeded by the hammering rhythms, their minds diverted by a spectacular run of guitar or piano—to have their attention caught, breathless, by glittering arpeggios.

Here, too, came Frank and Joyce.

Frank parked his middle-aged car on Broadway, empty and deserted at that hour of the night, and led the way into a dim sidestreet where yellow neon formed the outline of a trumpet; and green neon spelled out the name. There was no doorman, but a sidewalk awning shielded a cavernous, artificial stone entrance to a flight of stairs leading down. Sounds poured, in immodest fury, from the opening. Frank took Joyce's arm as they went down the steps. It was a flattering gesture, for her—Tony would never have thought of it. She said, "I'm not really dressed for this."

Frank said, "Nobody ever is."

Inside the lower door it was dim and cool. The dangling chandeliers were dimmed and brilliant amber spotlights, in the corners of the room, caught the brass flare of the trumpet with which a tall, lean, good-looking colored man sporting a tiny black mustache, was desperately trying to blow off the ceiling.

They stood there for a moment, taking in the silhouetted figures of men and women, strangely hushed and silent, leaning on tables in tense attention to the music. A waiter in black trousers and white shirt came over to them, "Good evening, Mr. Burdette." The accent was Italian.

"Hi, Louie. Got a table for me?"

"Of course, Mr. Burdette." He led the way to an empty table near the dais.

It pleased Joyce that Frank was known here. They sat down at the table and ordered drinks, and then Joyce tried to sort out the confusion of her senses. The music seemed, at first, almost, too loud to be distinguishable. A microphone, before the tall trumpeter, caught up the sound and carried it to twin loudspeakers mounted in the corners of the dais, making it louder still. The flaring spotlights seemed blinding on the white linen suits of the six musicians. The dark figures in the room behind their table seemed totally blacked out, so dark and silent were they. Almost, it seemed, she and Frank sat alone in a darkened room with only the musicians before them.

It was an intimate atmosphere, despite the numbers of people in the room.

Then other things began to come to her, as her mind became accustomed to the din. The hushed roar of an air-conditioning unit, the clink of glasses, the soft lights behind the bar in the rear of the room, strange cartoon-like murals on the walls—and over all, an odd smell that clung to everything and damped down the atmosphere.

It smelled, a little, like burning hay—old hay. But there was something else in the odor that made it different. It was a touch of sweetness that made the odor nearly pleasant—as though it were going to be a pleasant smell but had never quite achieved it and had stayed an unpleasant smell.

She asked Frank, "Do you smell something burning?"

"No, honey." He sniffed. "Smells fine to me."

After a while she gave it up and concentrated on the music. That's Jerry Best on the horn," Frank said. "Man on drums is Phil Schuyler. Piano is Don Willis. Clarinet, Frankie White, and the bass is Nutsie Burke. I don't know the other guy."

Joyce said, "Oh," with the proper reverence.

At first the music meant nothing, but then it began to come on her. It was hard, nervous music, underlaid with an exciting rhythm that first touched her lightly and then began to sink in, deeper and deeper, until it touched her pulse.

She looked at Frank sitting beside her, thinking, I didn't even know him until this afternoon, and now he seems so familiar, so close, so nice. He had put on the horn-rimmed glasses he wore in the office. She liked them. They aged his face, a little, but gave him an air of masculine authority. He looked a little like Ronald Colman playing a college professor—or something like that. His hair, she saw, receded a little from his forehead, giving him a widow's peak that added an exotic touch to his features. She watched his fingers, long and square-tipped, tapping cut the beat of the music, and wondered how it would feel to have those hands touching her.

But that was silly, of course. He was an older man, and how could he be interested in a kid. He was just taking you out tonight because he had nothing else to do. And yet, there was a thing she could feel about him—a sort of strength that grew out of his being older, and having an important job, and being a big man in Paugwasset. She started to compare him with Tony, but changed her mind. She didn't want to think about Tony, because she felt that she was doing something wrong to Tony by being here.

Abruptly the music came to an end. Jerry Best put down his horn and drew the microphone close to him. "Now, just take it easy, folks. Give us a few minutes to replace all that air we been blowing and we'll be right back."

Something clicked in the loudspeakers, and the musicians began to leave the stand.

Joyce saw that Frank had risen from his chair. "Hey! Jerry," he called. "Over here."

The lean negro turned, looking about, and then came toward them. "Hiya, man!" he said, thrusting out his hand. He called to the pianist, "Hey, Don. Dig this."

Wilson came over, his brown face and white teeth lit with a smile. "Frankie," Jerry said, "Where you been, man. Had us near flippin'. You get out there in the stix and we don't hear a word. Who's the chick?"

"Don, Jerry, this is Joyce Taylor. She works on my paper."

"Newspaper gal, hunh?" Wilson said. "Gimme five." He shook hands. It startled Joyce a little, seeing the big brown hand close around her small, white one. She had never touched a negro before, and was somewhat shocked that she felt no difference.

"Sit down for a while," Frank said. "Have a drink with us."

"No man. We want to light up."

"So get on in here!"

"Naw. It ain't cool here. Well cut on outside, C'mon with us. Louie'll hold your table."

Joyce said, "It seems cooler in here than outside?"

Frank laughed. "Not like that, Joyce. What he means is it isn't safe in here. All right, Jerry. We'll ask Louie to save the table."

Joyce followed the three men up the flight of stairs to the street. Frank said, "Where shall we go?"

"Over in the square," Jerry said. "Right over in front of NYU. Nobody bothers you there."

Joyce was puzzled. "What does he mean?" she asked Frank. "I don't understand a word he's saying."

"It's jive-talk. Musician's language. It's a sort of a short-hand talking," he said.

Frank was walking on one side of Joyce and Jerry on the other. Suddenly, shockingly, Jerry put his arm around her shoulder. It was so startling that she almost threw it off. Then she caught herself in time. Frank didn't seem to object and it must be all right. But . . .

"It's like this," Jerry said. "Musicians like to make all their noise with whatever they blow. Like you get kind of so you don't want to talk with words. So you make everything real simple for yourself? You dig?"

"I don't quite see . . ."

"Well, you don't have to look around for words you want. Like, I want to say, you like this? so I say, you dig it?" He hesitated. Then, to Frank he said, "Tell her, man," as though the burden of word-finding had been too much for him.

Frank asked, "You understood, didn't you?"

Joyce nodded her head. But that wasn't what she had meant. "Safe . . . Nobody bothers you . . . Light up . . ." But she was ashamed to ask any more questions, ashamed to reveal her ignorance.

The hulking buildings of the university towered dark and blank above them as they entered the bench-lined paths of Washington Square, and the greenery formed a dark tunnel over their heads. Don said, "Ain't Ginger over by the fountain?"

"Yeah," Jerry said. He took his arm from Joyce's shoulder. "You met my new chick, Frankie?"

"I think so. Ginger? Sure. Hey, Jerry, what happened to Bang Morley?"

"My old sax? Out!"

"Why? He was the greatest."

"Got on horse. I don't went nobody on hard stuff. Man that's dangerous. Junkie in the band with all that gauge around? Not for me."

"How's the new guy?"

"He ain't in the same groove. Got a different style like. But I dig him a lot more than Bang and all the time having to worry while he'd shoot the stuff. Man, I like to keep things cool." A girl, sitting on the concrete rim of the big central fountain stood up end came toward them, "Hiya, Ginger."

He went over to her and put his arm around her waist. Ginger had a light, almost golden skin, that glowed in the street lights. Joyce thought she was the most beautiful woman she had ever seen—for a colored girl. Then, after a moment, she amended that in her thoughts. Frank didn't think of people as colored or white, and—well, maybe she shouldn't. And, besides, Ginger was more beautiful than anyone she had ever seen.

They crossed the great open space of Broadway and sat down on a bench in the shadows of the trees.

Jerry pulled a cigarette case from his pocket, opened it and handed it to Ginger, who took one. Then he passed it to Frank. "Going to turn on, man?"

"Why not?" Frank took a cigarette and held it up to his mouth. Joyce thought it looked a little thinner than cigarettes ordinarily did. Don took one and passed the case back to Jerry.

"What about your chick?" Jerry asked. "Don't you want to light her up?"

"I'll have one," Joyce said.

"Wait a minute," Frank said, as Jerry started to pass the case. "You know what that is?"

"No. I—you mean . . ." Newspaper stories of jazz musicians floated through her mind. "Is it marijuana?" Her shocked voice startled them all to laughter.

Jerry said, "That's right, honey. That's the grass. It's the greatest."

Frank said, "Hey. Take it easy, Jerry."

"What's the matter, Frank? Will it hurt me?"

"No, honey. It won't hurt you. You haven't had any?"

"No. But . . ." It was important that she fit in. Maybe Frank wouldn't like her, if she refused. Maybe he would feel she was too young for him to take out. And suddenly it was desperately important that Frank should feel well-disposed toward her. Now, with Tony gone, there was no one. And besides she wanted to do what Frank was doing—to bring herself closer to Frank. "No," she said. "But I'd like to try it. May I have one?"

Jerry looked at Frank questioningly. "It can't hurt her," he said. "Never did anybody harm."

"I know," Frank said, "But . . ." He hesitated. "All right."

Jerry held out the case, and she drew one of the cigarettes from under the band. It was thinner than a regular cigarette. One end had a tiny, spiral twist, designed to hold the marijuana inside the thin paper roll. The other end was flattened, until only the paper remained. She started to put the spiraled end in her mouth.

"Not like that, honey. Watch me," Jerry said. He put the flattened end in his mouth, lighted the spiral with a quick touch of a match and without drawing on it When the tip was clearly aglow he drew the cigarette from his mouth. "Pinch a hole in one corner of the flat end with your nails—like this, and then press on the edge of the flat part so it makes a little hole." She followed his instructions carefully.

"Now, don't put the stick in your mouth. Make a mouth like whistling, and breathe in, holding it just in front of your lips." She did that, too, drawing in heavily. Suddenly the strong sweet odor, like burning hay, filled her throat and lungs.

"Don't cough, Joyce," Frank said. "The next puff wont seem so rough."

She drew again on the stick, more lightly, this time.

"Solid," Jerry said.

She took the stick down from her mouth. "What'll it do to me?"

"Maybe nothing," Frank said. "Some people it doesn't do anything to."

"But what's it like when it does do something?"

"There's only one thing charge does for you, honey," Jerry said. "It makes you feel good. That's all. Just good," He turned to Ginger. "This grass is great. The best. I dig it."

Joyce took two more drags on the stick, watching the little amber fire creep upward on the thin roll. The strange odor and unpleasant taste were gone now. It felt almost as though she were drawing very cold air into her chest. But nothing was happening. She said it. "Nothing's happening."

"Maybe it won't," Frank said, discouragingly.

"Will I do anything funny—I mean silly?"

"Of course not," Frank said. "It's not like liquor. You don't lose control or anything."

She drew again, still aware that it had no effect, then let her hand hang down holding the tiny cigarette. Suddenly she became aware of the night beauty of Washington Square Park. The cross atop the Judson church, glowing against the deep blue of the sky caught her eye, and the streetlamps against the facade of the arch. Each was a detail worth infinite attention. There was a faint, warm haze lying low against the ground, lending the whole park an atmosphere of unreality. Beyond the Square the lighted windows of a row of tall apartment buildings had a crystalline clarity—so clear were they that even from where she sat, nearly a sixth of a mile away, she could see well into the rooms, see the people moving about, see what they were doing.

It was as though every window of those huge apartment buildings were a stage on which a special performance was taking place for her benefit. Even the sky was richer and more velvety ease. How strangely wonderful and lovelier than any she had seen before, with deep-glowing blue stars—all warm and close and friendly—peering down at her. "God!" she said. "It's beautiful here." Then she remembered the stick and drew on it again. She turned to Frank, "But nothing's happening."

"Are you kidding?" he said. "No."

"Look around again. Here. Lean back against me." He put his arm around her shoulders as she sat on the bench and drew her close to him. Her skin was suddenly tremendously sensitive. She felt that she could count the individual strands of the wool in his sports jacket where it touched her shoulders. The warm breeze, more like July than May, caressed her skin, touched her instep, her toes, her ankles—slipped lithe fingers of air over her calves, fluttered her skirt and drifted upward over her thighs, passing over her stomach and chest like a sensual caress. Her body felt weightless, and her mind at complete rest.

Jerry said, "We got to get back for the next set, folks. You coming?"

Frank said, "We'll be along in a while."

"See you," Don said, and the three went off together. Joyce was hardly aware of their going, watching them as they walked through the archway of light formed by the trees. All they had become was part of the absolute, inutterable beauty of the park.

The important thing, though, was the feeling inside her—the wonderful, wonderful feeling. Now, as never before in her life, she felt safe, protected by Frank's arm about her. She snuggled closer against him, and his arm tightened responsively. It was like—like being in Daddy's arms, protected and safe and warm.

She turned, suddenly, and kissed Frank full on the lips.

6 ~ **Compulsion**

"What time did you get in last night . . ."

The sharp voice tore at the lovely fabric of the dream, shredding it into smoky tissues.

"Did you hear me, Joyce Taylor? What time did you get in?"

Slowly, with deliberate insolence, Joyce let herself come awake. She stretched luxuriously and yawned, half-rising on the bed to lend herself greater ease. The covers fell away from her; and there was another, immediate shrill outcry.

"Why aren't you wearing your nightgown?"

"Aunt Priscilla, can't you leave me alone?"

"What is the matter with you, Joyce. You've been acting like a maniac, and you've had that Thrine boy nearly frantic—calling me at one o'clock in the morning . . ."

"Oh! Tony."

"Yes, Tony," her aunt said.

"What did he say?" Joyce demanded, suddenly frightened.

"He didn't say anything. He just wanted to know if you had come home."

"What time is it?"

"Eight o'clock. Now tell me, what time did you get in last night?"

"Aunt Priscilla, I don't have the faintest idea. Does that satisfy you? Now I've got to get up." She started to scramble from the bed.

"Don't you dare get out of that bed. I'll get your robe for you. What will the neighbors think?"

"As far as I can see they won't think anything, since they can't see in. All right, give me the robe. I've got to hurry."

"And for what, may I ask?"

"I have an appointment for a summer job, and I have to be there at nine o'clock."

"Oh!" Priscilla Taylor was faintly mollified. "And how do you expect to hold a job if you keep this kind of hours."

"Don't worry," Joyce said. "I'll hold it all right." She was a little proud of the promptitude with which she had come up with this particular lie. Now it occurred to her that she could admit to working afternoons and Saturdays for the Courier preliminary to the end of the school year.

She showered and dressed as quickly as she could, coming downstairs to find her aunt sitting opposite the place on the table where Estelle had arranged her breakfast.

"I don't want any breakfast," Joyce said. "Just a cup of coffee."

"You sit right down and eat your breakfast," Priscilla said.

"All right." The fact was that she was almost starving. She remembered the huge meal she had eaten with Frank and Jerry and Ginger in the early morning before driving back to Paugwasset, and wondered if marijuana could have given her this voracious appetite.

After a while Priscilla said, "Do you or do you not intend to tell me where you were last night?"

"Oh, Aunt Priscilla, why carry on this way?"

"Have you been drinking?"

"No."

"Don't lie to me!"

"I don't care whether I do or not. But I wasn't drinking. You know I don't drink. You'd think from the way you talk I'd been doing something terrible, smoking marijuana or something." She suppressed the laugh that bubbled up inside her. The fact was that she felt particularly well this morning.

"I wouldn't put it past you," Priscilla said. "Well, if you won't tell me I'll just have to talk to that Thrine boy."

"Oh, all right. I had a fight with Tony yesterday so I went into New York last night with a couple of kids. We went to a late show at the Paramount."

"How did you go in?"

"Drove!" Her voice shrilled her impatience.

"Who with?"

"Charlie Case, if you must know—and his sister."

"Doesn't he have a junior license?"

"I don't know."

"Well, I'm sure he does, and he's not allowed to drive in New York."

"All right. Now I have to go." She rose from the table.

"Well," her aunt was weakening, "All right. But if you stay out like that again I'll just have to write and tell your father."

She caught the bus on the corner.

Frank Burdette came out of the front door of his house on Randolph Road wondering why he felt so much like a sinner. After all, looking back on it, he hadn't done anything wrong. What was there wrong with taking a girl to a night club. Nothing. And the marijuana? Nobody in all of history had ever been hurt by marijuana, at least to Frank's way of thinking. There were traps to the stuff, of course, as nobody knew better than Frank: psychological traps, the traps of getting to depend on the stuff to fill psychological needs—the way a person might get to depend too much on liquor or the movies. But there was all sorts of medical evidence to prove the stuff itself was harmless and non-habit-forming and that all the things usually said against it were no more than the meaningless nonsense of ignorance. Take the investigation once sponsored by New York's Mayor La Guardia, and that Academy of Medicine report . . . Oh, anyway, anyway, that wasn't it. Not the grass.

No. The trouble was the girl. Something about her touched him and held him. And *that* could assume the proportions of tragedy. After all, she was just a kid. A beautiful kid, with a body like a dream and a mind that maybe threw off sparks like Einstein on a hot night—but a kid. He turned the key in the lock and went down the steps.

Still, there was something about the way she cuddled up close to you, as though she trusted you—depended upon you for protection—that kind of caught at your heart and made you feel strong and wonderful. But you were a married man. You couldn't let this kind of stuff go to your head.

No. The solution was to have nothing to do with her. But she was working on the Courier. Could you keep the relationship on a nice impersonal basis?

Of course, you could fire her. But that would be a rotten trick. After all, she worked there last year for Harrigan and she did a good job, and yesterday she'd shown she could continue to do one. There was no legitimate reason for canning her; besides, it wasn't her fault if Frank found her attractive.

He waved good morning to George Gernert who was watering his front lawn, and a second later to George Jr. who was watering a corner of the lawn right through his romper.

He called, "Hey George! Junior's sprung a leak?"

And George called back, "Not again! That's the third time this morning."

That was the way to handle things, Frank decided, throwing back his shoulders and inhaling the fine air of early summer on Long Island. Just be firm and responsible and careful and friendly. Never let it get beyond being friendly, because that would be a terrible mistake.

All right, now. That was settled. And here came the bus. Frank stepped out from the curb and the bus pulled up. He got aboard, deposited his money in the receptacle and headed toward the seats. There was only one empty seat and—by heaven.

Oh, well. You couldn't make yourself look ridiculous and stand when the only empty seat was the one next to her. Frank sat down. "Good morning, Mr. Burdette."

"Not mister—remember?"

"Frank!"

"Lunch with me today?"

7 ~ Conflict

Tony swung the car around the corner and braked to a stop on Randolph Road in front of Burdette's house. He turned to Joyce on the seat beside him. She was leaning forward, adjusting her hair against wind-damage with the aid of the rear-view mirror.

"I don't see what you want to come here for," he said. "And I don't see any reason for dragging me along. Why should the city editor of the paper invite a copy girl to his house? After all, they're older people."

"If you don't want to come," Joyce said between clenched teeth that held a bobby-pin, "nobody's twisting your arm."

That caught Tony enough off base so that he lied. "Of course I want to," he said. "I want to spend a little time with you now and then. After all, I've hardly seen you this week."

His real purpose in coming had been to dissuade her. But now he allowed her to urge him out of the car.

Joyce said, "How do I look?"

She was a little worried about this. Frank had asked her to come tonight specifically to meet his wife, and it was not exactly the kind of thing she could approach easily. It brought to mind, somehow, one of those rare times when her parents had been at home. Her mother and father had planned to take her to New York. Mr. Taylor had driven downtown alone in the morning, and had then come home to pick them up. Joyce came out to meet the car and said—for some reason she had, by now, forgotten—"Daddy, Mother's not coming. She said for us to go ahead." And they drove off together.

She could not understand why this recollection kept to mind as they approached the front door. Unless it was because Frank had invited her to go to New York with him—although it might be better if she didn't mention it tonight. Since then, she had only had that one lunch with him during the week.

As they mounted the steps, Tony suddenly took fright. "Look, why don't you just go in alone. I'll only be bored with old people like them. I'm going. You go ahead and stay here." He released her arm and turned to go back down.

Tony!" Joyce hissed. "Don't you dare. You come right back here."

She seized his elbow and pulled him along with her. Janice Burdette opened the door to the bell. She stood slender and blonde, with an alert look about her blue eyes, and a set of features to which animation and intelligence lent a beauty beyond features themselves. She said, "Hello, Joyce. You are Joyce, aren't you? Of course. Frank said you would be here this evening, and I'm afraid it's my fault that Junior isn't in bed yet Come on in, and I'll whisk him off to dreamland."

In the middle of the living room floor a small boy, a very small boy with his little finger deeply intruded into his mouth, eyed the newcomers with a critical expression. He was standing a little straddle-legged, and the trap door of his pajama dangled open. Janice caught him up in her arms.

"You just sit down here, and Frank'll be right in. Frank! Frank! Company! Would you like a drink? Of course you would. I'll have Frank make you one while I stuff the by-product into his bed." She fled from the room trailing a wake of friendliness just as Frank came in.

Frank studied Tony Thrine as he performed the ritual of drink-making and strove, simultaneously, to keep up a flow of light, meaningless conversation. This was, of course, the cure that he needed. Once it was done—once this evening was over—he would see Joyce in her true perspective and she would see him. That was why he had insisted she bring Tony. Generation would belong to generation. Age to Age. And this would clearly point up the difference.

He counted on Janice to fall in with his plan—perhaps not knowingly but still to fall in with it. Her maturity would fit together with his, like matched parts of a whole, while Tony and Joyce would naturally go together. And then he would be rid of his obsessive interest in this—this kid.

Tony was a good-looking boy. You had to give him that. His dark hair was unruly, but not untidy. And at first, what seemed an entirely disjointed array of arms and legs and trunk on the divan became, on closer observation, a figure of graceful, feline ease—of total relaxation that could, catlike, instantly spring to action.

Then the most appalling thought struck Frank. He wondered if Tony had—that is, had known Joyce intimately, as a lover. After all, they were the right age for it. Nineteen, Joyce was. How old was Tony? Frank asked him.

"Eighteen," Tony said. "I'm just a year older than Joyce. We have the same birthday."

It was like a stick of dynamite going off in his brain, and Frank almost spilled the brace of highballs he was carrying over to the pair on the couch. Seventeen! Holy cow! And here he had almost . . . No. Hadn't thought of it for a second. Not a second. He rattled away furiously to conceal his shock. "You know, you two can get passes to anything you like. Movies. Even the major league ball games. After all, Joy—ce is a full-fledged newspaperwoman now." And then, "Where are you going to college, Tony?" Then, "I wanted to go to Harvard, too, when I was a kid." When I was a kid! Holy jumping Jesus! Look, Ma, I'm spinning.

The pressure had eased a little when Janice came back downstairs. She led the talk into feminine channels: clothes, travel, her trip to Maine on which she would leave tomorrow, how very easy was knitting once you got down to it, the latest rumor from Hollywood. It was amazing how easily Joyce and Janice got together. And yet, Frank thought he detected a certain tightness, as in the feeling-out thrusts of fencers, or the cautious sniffing of two suspicious dogs. But Janice was good. Really good. She could get along with anybody.

Like with Jerry. He remembered the first time Janice had met Jerry. He had always known Jerry—before high school, even. But Janice had never met a Negro socially before, and he could imagine her New England background really getting in the way the first time. But she had fallen right in the groove. Not a word about the tea, even. You expected these upcountry girls from Maine and places like that to be real prudish. But once he and Jerry had explained about it, she'd fallen right in. Once she got it straight that it wasn't even as bad for you as liquor— well, now she was a regular old viper, like anybody else. That was the difference between Janice and other girls . . .

Other girls? Hadn't Joyce taken it the same way. But Joyce was only a kid and he was thirty-one—and what the hell was he thinking about!

Janice said, "How do you feel about working on newspapers? Frank says you worked for the Courier last summer too, so I guess you must have made up your mind by now. Do you think you want to make a career of it?"

"I've been thinking about it," she said. "I guess I'm still a little young to get steamed up about it, but I'd like to work on newspapers for a while and then somehow get on a big magazine like Seventeen or Harper's Bazaar."

"I used to work for the Bazaar," Janice said. "I was an editorial assistant there. That's how I met Frank. We were both assigned to cover some demonstration of a new laundry machine. They always serve drinks at these press previews, and we both got a little tight and then he insisted on dragging me to some place in Harlem where he knew all the jazz musicians . . ."

Good old Janice, Frank thought. Consciously or unconsciously. She knew what she had to do, and was doing it.

He tried to get some kind of conversation going with Tony, but soon gave up. There was such an undercurrent of hostility, at least on Tony's part, that nothing could get started.

Then he heard Janice beginning something else, and a sensation of apprehension threaded up into his mind.

"Frank has covered some pretty big stories. Once he even made a hero of himself. The firemen—this was in Brooklyn—had been working on a tenement blaze and all the reporters—they get fire-line cards so they can get close enough to see and take pictures—the reporters were pretty close up to the building. A wall was about to come down, and everyone was being ordered to stand back, when Frank saw this child standing in the doorway of the wall that was going to crash. He yelled, 'C'mere, kid,' and started to run toward the child, but the kid was too frightened to do anything, and he had to go all the way up under that dangerous wall and grab the kid out of the doorway and start running back. He had just gotten out of the danger zone when the wall crashed down. He wouldn't write the story about himself—but the other reporters did, and it was in all the papers. But let me tell you something—That was the phoniest false modesty I ever saw, because he bragged to me about it for a week afterward . . ."

"I did not," Frank said. And everybody laughed. There was a sudden easing of the tension. Then Janice said, "Frank, why don't you show Joyce some of those stories. You've got them all in the scrapbooks upstairs, and I'll take Tony out in the garden. It's just beginning to be nice, Tony. I made Frank put the furniture out there while I was away, and you'll find it lovely and cool. I never saw a June like this. Why there are already fireflies in the yard, but no mosquitoes yet . . ."

This was the apprehension. This was what Frank had been fearing. He said, "No, Janice. She doesn't want to see those scrapbooks."

"Oh, but I do, Fra—M—Frank."

"Oh, come off it, now," Janice said. "Don't be such a phoney. Everybody knows you're dying to show them."

"I'd like to see them, too." Tony said—for obvious reasons.

"No you don't, young man," Janice said. "Who's going to keep me company in the yard? Besides, they wouldn't mean anything to non-newspaper people. You come along with me."

It was clear, Frank thought, how Janice's mind was working. She had sensed the trouble, taken steps to treat it, and now wanted them to be together so that the last vestiges could be swept away. But she was hurrying things too much. He didn't want to be alone with Joyce. Just didn't want to be alone with her yet. But what could he do now?

"All right. Joyce, come upstairs with me so I can show you what a big shot I am."

Tony and Janice carried their drinks out through the dining room and kitchen into the back yard. Frank watched Joyce climbing the stairs ahead of him. She caught the full skirt of her light dress high on one thigh so that it would not interfere with her feet. The gesture charmingly shaped her figure under the light fabric.

"The books are in the bedroom—to the left." he said. His throat felt tight and dry. His voice came almost as a whisper. "Careful. Don't wake Junior."

In the bedroom she sat down on the spread, leaning back on her arms. Her skirt spread out fan-wise on the tufted chenille. Her attitude emphasized the freshness of her youth.

He thought: Cut it out, Frank! Stop it! Get control of yourself, man.

Through the open, screened window overlooking the yard and the garden came the murmur of voices, Janice's and Tony's, blended with the tinkle of the little concrete fountain full of goldfish that Frank had, himself, installed last fall.

There was a vanity, on one side of the room, cluttered with the miscellaneous appurtenances of feminine charm: bottles of cream, ointments, nail polish; a jar full of bobby-pins; brushes, combs, a silver-backed mirror engraved with the initials JB; there were nail-buffers, emery boards, scissors, a single fastener from a garter belt, eyeshadow boxes, tweezers, a compact and hosts of other items.

Facing the vanity, but across the room, stood a bureau, with the male equivalents of these beauty aids—lotions, hair tonic, after-shave talc—the array perhaps a little neater because Janice was committed to restoring order to whatever chaos Frank might create, but felt no such responsibility toward her own things.

And against the wall, between the two windows that looked out on the back yard, hunched a desk—a very wreck of a desk, teetering on spindling legs of oak which supported a bookshelf before reaching up to maintain the inclined face of the drop-leaf and the frame. The shelf was loaded down with scrapbooks.

Tensely, insistently, Frank bent down and picked up three, bringing them back to where Joyce was seated on the bed. He seated himself next to her and opened one book across their two laps.

His voice trembling, his grip on himself slipping, he tried to tell her the story behind each yellowed clipping.

Suddenly Joyce turned to him, looking up at him with her great somber eyes. "Frank," she whispered, the faint sound of her voice merging with those from the window. "Frank, do you love me?"

He bent, quickly, and kissed her lightly on the forehead, feeling his whole body trembling. But he said, "Of course I do, honey. Now, this story began when . . ."

"No, Frank. I mean, really."

His mind cast about frantically, but all control was gone now. There was nothing to seize upon which could protect him from his own burning hunger. The books fell to the floor as he caught her to him and felt the response of her warm, excited lips. She trembled against him, and her fingers dug deep into the flesh of his back.

Something, very like fire, seemed to be consuming them . . .

8 ~ Substitution

For Joyce the romance with Frank had always the added poignancy of impending tragedy.

The first blow fell that same night—the night she shared ecstasy with Frank, while Frank's wife and Tony talked together in the garden below.

The rest of the evening had gone off, somehow, in a state of continuing tension. Tony was hurt and angry because Joyce had deserted him. Frank was tormented by his own guilt—faced with the horrifying realization that he had against his will succumbed to a girl only a little more than half his age. Janice, her plans all made to depart for Maine with the baby the following morning, was openly bewildered at the tensions of the others, and still more bewildered by a psychic unease, that told her something had gone dreadfully wrong.

But the real blow came later, when Tony and Joyce had muttered "good nights" and "thank yous" to Frank and Janice in the doorway of the little house on Randolph Road, and had gone out to the parked car at the curb.

They got in and Tony, jaw grimly set, started the motor.

"It was fun, wasn't it?" Joyce said. It wasn't what she meant. She meant glorious, wonderful, tremendous. But these were not words she could say. A man loved her, wanted her—would protect her. Frank was strong and able and adult. He was already a father, the very symbol of adulthood. He was successful, mature.

Tony said nothing.

"What's the matter with you?" she demanded.

He put the car in motion, driving down Randolph Road like a man escaping demons. At Central Avenue he forced the rebellious vehicle around the curve with a mad squealing of tires on the macadam.

After that, the convertible shot through the moonlit darkness, a thunderbolt of whistling winds and whirring motor in the silence of the night. Past the big, silent houses on Central Avenue, past the recurring streetlamps, past the end of the macadam where the street became a highway and turned to concrete paving, past the new development in South Paugwasset.

"Tony!" she said. "Where are you taking me?" In the dim lights from the dashboard, his face was brewing a storm of violence. "Answer me!" Still the car sped on. "Tony, you stop this car right this minute."

No answer.

"If you don't let me out of this car, I'll . . . I'll . . ." Sudden hysteria gripped her. She caught at the doorhandle, pressed downward and tried to force it open against the flying wind-stream. Tony reached over with one hand, not taking his eyes from the road, and caught her wrist with steely fingers, pulling her back into the car. Then he reached past her and pulled the door to full latch. After that, as though nothing had interrupted him, he drove forward into the night, faster and faster, until the whipping airstream lashed Joyce's unfastened hair down in stinging blows against her face. Suddenly she dropped her face into her hands, and sobs jerked at her shoulders.

"What are you doing, Tony?" she wailed. "Please, Tony."

Then he stopped the car, pulling it up sharply like a horse that is forced to rear, on the shoulder of the road.

The silence, after the roaring of wind and motor, was poignant, almost unbearable. Then, one by one, the night-sounds of the country insistently made themselves heard. Crickets in the tall grass that bordered the highway. A nightbird "hooooo-ed" in the distance, and somewhere ahead a late train on the Long Island railroad clicked its electric way over an untidy roadbed. Water gurgled faintly through a culvert, and leaves, lightly displaced in the gentle breeze, rustled softly.

Tony drew a pack of cigarettes from his pocket, offered it to Joyce and, when she refused, lit one for himself.

The girl stared at his grim face, she was frightened. Tony was never like this.

"Joyce," he said, suddenly, "are you in love with Burdette?"

She stalled, "What?"

"I asked if you are in love with—with that editor?"

"Don't be silly." Was that the right tone? Should she have said: Don't be ridiculous? Or: What are you talking about?

"He's a lot older than you are, Joyce." He wasn't saying it flatly. His voice was flat, but something underlay the flatness, as though he were keeping, by a tremendous effort, from breaking into sobs.

"Oh, stop talking like a child."

"I'm your age, Joy. If I'm a child, so are you."

"Girls mature earlier than boys."

"I've heard that before. It all depends on which girls, what boys."

"You'd better stop this nonsense and take me home."

"No, Joy. This is too important for us to just shrug off. If I find out that you're—you know I saw you last Friday with Frank."

"I don't care what you saw, and don't you dare threaten me."

"I'm not threatening you, Joy; I'm just telling you what I'm going to do if things turn out the way I suspect."

"You are absolutely the stupidest boy I've ever met."

"Keep it calm, Joy. We're not fighting. We're just clearing up some confusion."

Desperately she wished that Frank were here. Frank was a man, full-grown and protective. Strong, wise. He loved her and would defend her from—from this kid who had rejected her when she had needed him. She forgot that it was she who had really done the rejecting. "Well, let's clear it up then," She felt so much older and stronger than Tony.

"I don't know how you feel about it, but after last week, I feel that you belong to me, and it's up to me to look out for you. If you broke off with me for some other kid, that'd be all right I wouldn't be happy about it, and I'd probably make a big fuss, but it wouldn't be wrong—like this is."

"What on earth are you talking about?"

"Tm talking about Frank, and you know damned well I am. Joyce, you're too young to get involved with an older man, like that. He's married. He's got a wife and kid. Can't you get it through your stupid head that you'll ruin your life with that guy. Even if he loves you, he doesn't want to love you. He's—oh, hell, I don't know what he is, but he's not for you. And if I find out you're going too far with him—I'll tell your aunt. You know what she'll do."

Then the idea came to her. She forced her voice to a calm. "Tony, you know better than what you're saying." There was only one way to convince him. And, for one blinding moment, she saw herself as a martyr, sacrificing herself at the stake for her love.

She moved closer to Tony. "I'll show you who I love, Tony." She had to do something. If her aunt found out about Frank, she'd probably have him arrested, have him run out of town. She put her lips to Tony's and kissed him.

Frank and Janice went to bed that night like two strangers who, by chance, have been forced together into a shipboard stateroom. Janice was troubled because of something she could not bring into the forefront of her consciousness. She knew that something had happened which threatened her; knew too that some part of her had understood it fully and was weighing it; taking measures for her protection from it—she knew, too, that whatever had happened had lowered a veil of estrangement between herself and her husband. But what, exactly, it was that had happened she did not know, could not let herself guess.

But Frank's problem was far greater. He *knew* what had happened. Worse still, he knew that it would happen again and again. He loved Janice. She was his wife, the mother of his child, a capable, wonderful person on whom he could depend for everything he needed. But something about this strange kid, this seventeen-year-old *femme fatale,* had caught him in a terrible grip.

She was beautiful, intelligent, sensuous—but that wasn't quite it. Nor was it the tense, passionate excitement she roused in him. That, too, was mere seasoning for the dish. No. There was something else she gave him, something not quite healthy—not for either of them. A kind of unquestioning obedience. A slavish devotion to his orders and desires which flattered him and made of him more than he was, but which at the same time gave him virtually an incestuous feeling, like that of, say, a father over-affectionate with his daughter.

He looked across the room at Janice, brushing her soft, ash-blonde hair before the mirror. He couldn't let such a thing happen again. It must never happen again. What did a man want out of life more than Janice gave. All right, she had moods. All right, she had a mind of her own—and could raise utter hell with it, too. But he and Janice were two parts of the same whole—perfectly matched, perfectly mated. He wished she were not leaving tomorrow to be gone for the whole summer.

She was wearing a pale, transparent gown of green nylon or silk, or something, and the soft light of the small lamp on her vanity outlined the lovely shape of her legs. He thought, how can you get excited over any woman but her, lovely Janice, his Janice.

"Janice," he said softly. "Honey." She did not turn and he could not see her face. What was she thinking? Did she know? "Baby," he said. "Turn out the light and come here."

There was a click, and he saw her pale figure coming to him across the room in the faint, leaf-spotted moonlight seeping through the window.

Then she was in his arms, her lips parted and pressed to his, and he tasted the salt of her tears.

Joyce undressed slowly, her whole body aching with exhaustion. Her dress she let fall to the floor. Her arms hurt. She looked in the mirror. Her shoulders and neck and upper arms felt bruised, but they showed no marks. She stretched the rubber waistband of her panties, let them drop to her feet, stepped out with one foot and with the other kicked them onto a chair. Her hair was wild with the slip stream of the convertible and she had no energy left to brush it. She went to the bathroom and washed away the lipstick smears around her mouth—but nothing could wash away the smear inside her. She started to the closet for her nightgown, thought of the vast energy that would require, and turned back to the bed, pulled down the sheet and single blanket and slipped in.

What's the matter with me?

She pressed the convenient switch that turned off the light over the bed and tried to settle herself for sleep.

Why did I do it?

She fluffed up the pillows and shifted her head, then turned and tried the other way, but there was no rest in her.

She thought, how could you do such a thing? How could anybody let themselves get like that? What was wrong with a person who behaved like that? What was it old Iris had said, ". . . you need psychiatric help . . ." Was that it? Was she crazy?

She remembered things in school. Defiance. That had been the thing. Why did she have to write a shocking paper when everyone else was satisfied with things like measles and virus pneumonia? Why had she insisted on smoking in the school corridors between classes? After all, she hadn't actually needed a smoke. Why had she tried that idiotic dance during the auditorium study period? That was so stupid, so meaningless, so ridiculous except as defiance. Or was defiance the whole story? Wasn't it also something else, almost as if you were courting disaster, searching for trouble, demanding punishment?

And the afternoon, just one day over a week ago, right after Dean Shay had kicked you out of school—what had happened that you *had* to tempt Tony so disgracefully? Supposing you got—got yourself with child? Was that it? Was that the trouble you were courting this time? Or was there still something else?

She remembered it another way, then. There had to be someone. You had to belong to someone, be someone's property, so they would take care of you and keep you safe, because people did take care of the things that belonged to them, didn't they?

And then, when Tony was so angry, why shouldn't you have gone out with Mr.—with Frank. And everything had been so wonderful—the fine, safe feeling, the protected feeling of being with a grown man.

But tonight—first one and then the other. Betrayer. Delilah. First betraying Tony with Frank, and then Frank with Tony. Awful—but just wonderful, wonderful, the feeling of being loved. And two loves were better than one.

Now she belonged to two men, but it was horrible. No, wonderful. No . . .

Tony drove his car into the garage, switched off the lights and climbed out closing the garage doors behind him. The moonlight cast long shadows over the lawn, making it look vast and deep and mysterious, and the huge darkened house where his father and mother lay sleeping loomed like a castle out of a fairy tale. He walked over to the grape arbor and seated himself on the long bench that ran the length of it.

There was something wrong with Joyce—something he would have to figure out. Maybe, if he were to write to her parents—but no, you couldn't do that. There was honor among kids. You couldn't betray that.

And for a while—he took out a cigarette and lit it—he had thought she was getting herself into trouble with that Frank Burdette. No. Nothing like that could happen. Frank was too nice a guy. And he had a wife and kid, and that kind of thing just didn't happen. Besides, he knew better now—after the way she had demonstrated, in the car, her ardent regard for him.

Still, it was too bad Joyce couldn't graduate. After all, what could her aunt do to her? Nothing. She'd just yell a little and then go to the school, and yell some more, and then Joyce would be back in and she'd graduate. Why couldn't she face the consequence of what she'd done? But then, there was always something a little funny about Joyce. Not that it made any difference with him, Tony.

You had to take the bad with the good in another person, and things couldn't always be your way.

Then he indulged himself in a moment of tender dreaming about Joyce—about the fact that she was his girl and everything was going to be all right.

He tossed away his cigarette, then, seeing the spark still glowing on the lawn, got up from the bench and stepped on the butt. Then he went into the house.

9 ~ Flight

Even the single crisis Joyce had feared she easily managed to evade by a quick fabrication. She had been terrified that her aunt would insist on attending the graduation exercises. But her aunt's interest was not really that deep. When Joyce told Priscilla that she had decided not to participate in the commencement exercises, the older woman had been more than pleased at the assurance she would not have to cope with that additional burden.

Priscilla Taylor was not a lazy woman, but a tired one. The comfortable income her brother provided in return for her care of Joyce was not enough to make up for the life which had somehow slipped by her, but it did ease the struggle to maintain the struggle. Once Priscilla Taylor had harbored a desire to have a life of her own, a husband of her own, a home of her own. Now, the money provided by her brother was an excuse for abandoning the desire, and she had reached the age where she had convinced, herself that she preferred things as they were.

Joyce never understood this mechanism—but she regarded its effects as all to the good.

At the Courier she had progressed. At first tentatively, and later because it had proved practical, Frank had given her minor assignments to fulfill. Once, when Lew Myron had 'phoned in sick, he had sent her in Lew's stead to cover a meeting of the Community Welfare Society, and her tense anxiety to satisfy had resulted in a more than routine story on the normally tedious.

Then he tried her on day police court. She had covered the routine arraignments with the elaborate attention to detail of a proceedings-reporter for the Congressional Record, and the enthusiasm for color of a *Time*-staffer.

So Frank gave her a raise, and told her she could call herself a reporter—although copy traffic was still her proper province.

As the summer wore on, Frank took her repeatedly to the Golden Horn, to the Stuyvesant Ball Room where the greatest of Dixieland musicians held forth weekly in the best New Orleans tradition, to Jimmy Ryan's, to Birdland, to the Three Deuces, to all the places where he was known by the musicians as a connoisseur of jazz. He introduced her to players, famous and infamous, and took a strange pride in the way she took to them and their music, and the way they took to her.

Cautiously, for fear of the police and not for fear of any other consequences, he further taught her the use of marijuana. Solemnly he steered her away from the junkies, users of heroin and cocaine, and solemnly explained the perils of those drugs with a "hook."

"Look," he told her one night when she asked why he regarded marijuana as so right, heroin as so wrong, "heroin has a hook. It's a narcotic. If you take it once you only need a little tiny bit to get high, and it'll give you a lift that takes you right through the ceiling. But the next time you come around it won't do the same thing for you unless you take a little bit more, and, every time you use it if you go at it regularly, you've got to keep adding to the dose. Pretty soon you need two capsules, then three, then five, just to get your regular kick. All right, that might not do any harm. But, suppose you take three caps or five for several days running. One morning you wake up and find you're clean. You can't put your hands on any. Suddenly you get into a panic, because you've got to have it. You chase all over hell and gone looking for it and you don't find it. After a while that panic wears off. Then you get it again, and you're more cautious. You get enough for a longer stretch, and you hoard it carefully. When you come to the end of that supply you're desperate. You'll sell your soul for more. You can't eat. You can't think. You can't do anything but hunt for heroin." He looked at her. "Remember Bang Morley?"

Joyce shook her head.

"Well, Bang was one of the greatest sax men that ever lived. He used to be with Jerry Best. He could do things with a sax that would curl your hair. He started off sniffing heroin—inhaling it up through his nose through a rolled up dollar bill from a little card where he'd spill the powder. At first that was all right. Made him feel like the king of the band. Then it began to get him. He couldn't play as well. His mind was always taken up with where he could get more of the stuff. Jerry offered to pay for a cure for him, but he wouldn't take the cure. He was too much bound up in the stuff. He stopped showing up for work and finally Jerry had to fire him. Yesterday I read in the

News that he took a flying jump off the Empire State Building."

Joyce said, "Oh," with a quick little indrawn breath of horror. Then she said, "You're just playing games, Frank. Isn't marijuana just as bad?"

Frank shook his head. "As far as anybody has ever been able to tell, marijuana can't hurt a fly. I don't say it's good. It isn't. Anybody who needs marijuana, or liquor or anything else, such as coffee or cigarettes, to get along in the world—well, there's something wrong with that guy. But marijuana doesn't have a hook. If you can't get it— okay, you can't get it. You wish you had it, then you forget about it. You never lose control of yourself in tea, the way you do, for example in liquor. It doesn't load you down. It doesn't damage your body or your brain. I told you—the New York Academy of Medicine once checked up on that. But good for you? No, it isn't good for you. I know a lot of people who try it and don't like it. The significant thing is, they are always people I'd call mentally healthy. They're the really sane people I know . . ."

Joyce learned about other things from Frank. He introduced her to classical music, explaining that the channel through which it could be approached was the same channel which led to jazz—good jazz. He brought her to books, to Chinese food, to modern painting. He introduced her to long, rambling, conversational walks through the byways of Manhattan. He showed her Harlem and the Williamsburg Bridge. He took her to Coney Island and the Lewisohn Stadium. Together they saw ball games, went for a moonlight swim at Jones Beach.

And in time Joyce learned that Frank was jealous of Tony . . .

One day he said, "Joy? Every once in a while I see you with that kid Tony Thrine. Do you still go out with him?"

"Sometimes. Don't you like him?"

"Oh, sure. Nice kid. But he drives like a maniac."

"Don't be silly, Frank. Tony's a terrific driver."

"You know best," he said. "But I don't care much for the way he cuts through traffic. He's going to get himself in a sling one of these days."

"Frank, you aren't jealous are you?"

"Don't be dopey, kid. I'm never jealous of anybody. But I wish you wouldn't ride around with him in that car so much."

"But I don't ride with him much. I hardly ever go out with him."

"Aw, forget it." Then, after a moment, he said, "Joy, do you have to wear that dress?"

"What's wrong with it?"

"Nothing. Nothing at all."

"Then why did you mention it?"

"Because I hate to see you wearing things in poor taste."

"What are you talking about, Frank. I've worn this lots of times and you never said anything."

"I know. But it's cheap looking. You look like a small town brat trying to look like a loose woman. Don't wear it again when you're going out with me."

And by his anger she understood that he was not put out about the dress, but about Tony.

Joyce was seeing Tony, all right. Sometimes once a week, sometimes twice. If she had asked herself why, she would have said it was because every once in a while she wanted to get out with somebody her own age— somebody who wasn't constantly teaching her things and forcing her to be older than she was.

But she was being pretty intimate with Tony as well. Not always. Not very often. But sometimes. He lacked Frank's maturity, sophistication, sensual tenderness; but his fumbling excitement was sometimes more edifying to Joyce's soul. She could not tell exactly why or how, or what made it that way, but Tony was very important to her. She told herself that she was being sweet to him only to prevent him from suspecting Frank, from spilling the beans to her aunt who would cause trouble for Frank.

But in her heart she realized that she wanted Tony to love her, just as she wanted Frank to love her. She wanted love, love above all—the certainty of male affection.

After a time she became inured to the subtle tensions, the two-way stretch of the problem. She settled into the calm of being the beloved of two men as though it were as normal as corn flakes for breakfast.

Then, in mid-August, the final blow fell . . .

Frank left his house, that morning, at peace with the
world and with himself. Even the burning heat of the August sun, glaring on the black macadam, could not interfere with the great calm that lay on his soul. The Managing Editor, old Force Dutney, had increased his salary and
he was, this afternoon, to collect his first paycheck. Moreover, an article which he had written on tea-smoking had
been accepted, the day before, by Esquire Magazine.

God was in his familiar heaven, and Frank Burdette was
getting along just fine.

Then he met the postman.

"Hi, Mr. Burdette," the little gray man said. "Don't have
much for you this morning. Just this one letter here.
Guess it's from your wife."

"Thanks, Mr. Main," Frank said. "Beautiful day, isn't it?"

" 'Sall right if you're in an air-conditioned office, I
guess," Mr. Main said, thereby revealing the smallness of
his soul and his inability to appreciate the glories of nature. "But, as a carrier of the mail, I kind of prefer au-
tumn. Well, see you tomorrow." He hitched the bag a little higher on his shoulder and plodded up the street.

Frank turned the letter over, as though something new
could be revealed by Janice's familiar script on the envelope, then put it in his pocket. He would read it in the office. Nothing should be permitted to distract him from the
loveliness of nature this fine August morning.

He did not get to the letter until just before lunch. Then
he opened it read the first few lines, put it down, rose to
close the ever-open door of his office, and returned to the
neat, tight script.

My dearest fuzzyhead:

*I can see from your few letters that you are terribly
unhappy, and I wish with all my heart that I knew some
way to help you.*

*This has happened before, I know. But never like this.
I knew, even before I went away, that it was a mistake
for me to go.*

*It's very hard for me to write this—because it means
admitting it to myself as well. But I did see it before I
left, and your letters say it over and over again be-*

tween the lines, even if they don't say it overtly. I'm only putting it down like this so you'll know I understand the facts—not just know them. It's very important, my darling, that you see the difference between understanding and knowing.

You've been having an affair with that lovely little Taylor girl. I don't blame you for it. Every year I go off like this and leave you alone with no one to keep you company and I guess—like it says in the old saying—a man isn't made of wood. I could say that I don't mind, but it wouldn't be true. The thought of you intimate with another girl makes me frantically jealous. Fortunately, for me, I don't really know this in the literal sense. It just kind of comes to me from what you write in your letters. And she is very beautiful. It's like putting two and two together and then saying, well, I won't add them up so I only suspect they make four.

I wouldn't write you like this if it were just for the affair you're having. You've had these summer affairs before. But there is something else. You're probably concealing it from yourself, but you're terribly unhappy without her, and jealous and angry with yourself. That shows in your letters, too. And if you let yourself get more deeply entangled in the emotional problems this thing is making for you, you'll become so involved with the Taylor girl that I'll never get you back.

I don't like to threaten you, my darling. And this isn't really a threat, because I'm so sure of the outcome. But, my darling, you must decide now, before things become worse. You are supposed to come up here the eighteenth anyway, so let's make that the time for decision—a sort of cutting-day for the Gordian knot.

Don't come here, my darling, unless you have finished off this affair. Please don't come. And if you don't come, then I'll know that it's all over and that it has been wonderful being married to you, but that we had to break it off.

And, if you do come, I shan't say a word to you. Not a word, my darling. But I'll know that you love just me . . .

P.S. Junior slobbered on the letter. He means he loves you, too.

Joyce met Tony at the corner of Second Street and Madison. She had intended to go with Frank to New York, that evening. But all day long he had been in a strange, tense mood. At noon she had seen him close the door of his office, a thing he never did ordinarily, and he had kept it closed until late in the afternoon.

She had been supposed to have lunch with Frank, but he did not open the office door, did not come out, as he ordinarily would, to ask if she was ready. Finally she had gone by herself. About four o'clock he came to her desk.

"Listen, Joy," he said. "Something's come up, and I won't be able to make it tonight. There's something I have to get straightened out here." And that was when she decided to telephone Tony.

"Want to take me out tonight?"

"Why not? Don't I always?"

"So pick me up at the corner of Madison and Second at six o'clock, Okay?" Tony's car was parked on Madison, just above where it narrowed for the underpass beneath the Long Island Railroad bridge.

She waved at him as soon as she saw him, his spidery legs mysteriously entangled in the steering wheel, his arms stretched back behind his head as he reclined in luxurious ease against the leather seat cushions.

"Hi, lazy," she said.

"Saving up my energy for school," he said. "It's been decided. I'm not going to Harvard at all. I'm registered at NYU. Went in to town this morning to get signed up."

"Good," Joy said. Not really meaning anything special.

"Any particular place you want to go?" Tony asked, as he started the car.

"I got eyes for some sea-food."

"What kind of an expression is that? I've got eyes for some sea-food?"

"It's musicians' talk," Joyce explained. "Jive-talk. All the cats dig it. You mean you ain't hip, man?"

"Cut it out."

"What do you mean, cut it out? I'll talk as I please."

"Not with me, you won't," Tony said. "And another thing, why did you tell me to meet you at the corner of Second and Madison? What's the matter with in front of the Courier building? You do still work there, don't you?"

"Of course I do."

"Then . . .?"

"Well . . ." She stumbled. "I—I had something I had to see about at the corner of Second and Madison."

"Something important at the ice house, of course . . ." His voice was loaded with sarcasm.

"As a matter of fact, it was. I had to see a Mister—Mister Pelley there. It was about an—an Elks meeting."

"Quit lying to me, Joy."

"Don't you dare call me a liar, Tony Thrine. If you ever say that again I'll . . ."

"Just what will you do, Joy?"

"I'll never see you again."

"All right. Now I'll tell you a few things. The reason you didn't want to meet me in front of the Courier building is because you didn't want Frank to see you riding off with me. And the reason you didn't want him to is because you've been lying to him just the way you've lied to me. And if you've been lying to him about going out with me, then you've been lying about how—how close we are. And if you've been lying about that, you've been lying because you were close with him and you couldn't let him find out about anybody else—just like you couldn't let me. Is that true?"

"How can you talk like that?"

"How could I not have before? That's the real question. There're a couple other deductions I can make, too. I'm just a kid. Joy, but I'm a smart kid, and you aren't so darned brainy you can put it over on me all the time."

"But it's not true, Tony. I swear it's not."

"All right. There's a simple way to test it. We'll drive to Mr. City Editor Burdette's house, and we'll walk in, and I'll ask him."

"You can't."

"Of course I can."

"Think how it would embarrass me."

"I am thinking. And that's just what we're going to do. You've been putting it over on both of us, and I'm not going to stand for it any more. Either we see Burdette, or I know I'm right and it's all over between us. How about it?"

For long minutes Joyce sat silent on the seat of the moving car.

"You can't decide. All right." He swung the car into a street "We'll go to Burdette's."

"No, Tony!" Joyce was crying.

"Don't give me that sob-stuff, Joy. What's it going to be? Will you admit it, or do we go there."

"All right. I admit it. Now take me home."

Tony said nothing. Grimly he drove through the tree-lined streets, all golden and shadow-striped in the setting sun, grimly stopped the car before the Taylor house, set back from the street among its landscaped lawns.

Joyce got out of the car without a word, and stepped across the grass island to the sidewalk. Then she turned to look at Tony. "I hate you," she said, and started to run across the lawn.

"Joy!" Suddenly he could forgive her anything. She half-halted. "Joy!" Then his anger got the better of him. "Go to hell," he said. He jerked the car into low gear and, racing the engine, took off

It was not until the following evening that she had an opportunity to talk to Frank. He stopped by her desk in the morning. "Want to come to the house tonight?"

"Of course." She smiled up at him.

"Good kid," he said, patting her hand, and went on to his office.

That evening they rode uptown together on the bus, but Frank said nothing. Something strange and intangible seemed to have come between them, and it frightened her. She needed Frank, now, needed him desperately.

When they reached the house Frank unlocked the door and let her pass into the hallway. "Let's go out in the kitchen and get something to eat."

"No, Frank. Not yet." She came up close to him, her face tilted up to his. "Frank, darling," she said, her voice husky. "I want you."

Suddenly, almost angrily, he caught her in his arms, crushing her to him. He lifted her in his arms and carried her up the stairs.

Afterwards, she told him.

"I had to be good to him, Frank. Honest I did. He would have told my aunt, and would have—I don't know what she would and you know what he would have done."

"It's all right, honey. I understand." He kissed her tear-streaked face.

The envelope was lying on her desk when she arrived at the Courier next day, and the door of Frank's office was closed. It was addressed to Miss Joyce Taylor, in a hand-writing she recognized from memos and notations on copy.

She looked about her to see if anyone was watching. But the scattering of people in the office were bowed over their typewriters, each with its continuous roll of yellow copy paper mounted on the back, or closely attending to the long strips of manila paper on which they were mark-ing the strange hieroglyphs of the copyreader.

She opened the letter and read it through, then read it through again. It was the same, both times—a short, typewritten note.

Joyce:

I have gone to Maine to spend two weeks with Janice and Junior. When I come back, I hope we will both have forgotten the things that happened this summer. Please do not misunderstand me. You are a wonderful person—far too good for me, in fact. But Janice needs me and, in a funny way, I guess I need her.

Go back to Tony. He's a fine boy, and he does love you, no matter how angry he may be now.

Don't quit the paper. You're going to make a terrific newspaper woman. And by the time I get back, you'll see, this whole thing will have worked itself out.

So long,
Frank

That night Joyce packed her things in the stillness of her bedroom. In the morning she waited until her aunt had left the house to go shopping. Then she called a cab, went to the bank where she had deposited her earnings from the Courier, and withdrew all her money while the cab waited. Then she went to the station and caught the 11:20 for New York.

Part Two

THE HORSE

With phantoms and unprofitable strife,
And in mad trance, strike with our spirit's knife
Invulnerable nothings. . . .
PERCY BYSSHE SHELLEY

Joyce went to see Jerry Best as a last resort.

She had thought about it a long time—perhaps an hour or so during each of five or six evenings—before she actually got on the subway and rode downtown to Washington Square.

For a while, before that, she had been able to kid herself that things were going very well. For anyone else but Joyce Taylor, in fact, they would have going well indeed. But the desperate forces that drove her demanded something beyond the simple successes of employment, food and a place to live.

She had spent almost no money at all during the summer of work on the Courier, and it had not been hard to get a job—theoretically an editorial job—before her reserves ran out. She was, officially, an assistant editor on the *Machine Tool Journal*, a publication devoting itself to internal grinders, lathes and other subtle mechanisms of the early atomic age. Behind her official title she concealed the fact that she was one of four employees of the publisher, the others being a myopic baldhead with the entirely surprising name of Eugene Tip, the editor; a stenographer named Myra Feldman, who lived in Brooklyn and had designs on a genuine dentist, and an advertising manager-cum-bookkeeper who hid behind the pseudonym Chauncey Scott Arvin, and was altogether too glorious a person for the *Machine Tool Journal.*

Her duties were multitudinous and tedious, requiring only a minimum of intelligence—that is, just a trifle more than that possessed by Miss Feldman whose perfunctory performance of them before had necessitated hiring Joyce. She was in charge of mailing out cards inducing manufacturers to provide information on new products, in charge also of the measurement of type, the production of cuts, the reading of galley proofs, and the fetching of innumerable containers of coffee for Eugene Tip—who took his eminent position with great seriousness.

Her salary had been thirty-five dollars a week, and within a month had climbed to forty-five, to the scandalized amazement of Miss Feldman who, after two years of unremitting indolence, was earning only forty.

Thus, in things material, Joyce was a success. But Joyce had conceived of glittering Manhattan as a gay round of night clubs and orchids, an orgy of parties and diaphanous nightgowns, and in this direction she had failed miserably. Mistakenly assuming that she needed, above all things, freedom, she had rented a furnished room instead of going to a girls' residence hotel. She understood that YWCAs and the like prohibited male companionship, and failed to apprehend that acquaintance with women often is requisite to acquaintance with men . . .

For men were what Joyce needed.

She had been thinking about Jerry and Don and Ginger and the boys in the band for a long time—but not thinking of seeing them. An unconscious residue of prejudice—which even the months with Frank had not entirely overcome—would not allow her to think of herself as a girl whose only friends in all the great city of New York were colored.

But as September turned to October, and October to November, it became more and more clear to her that she must, must, must make human contacts other than with the trio of gay souls who produced the *Machine Tool Journal.* The mad round of cinema palaces had now so far palled that she could summon no shadow of sympathetic passion for Gary Grant or Van Johnson, Bing Crosby or Montgomery Clift. No longer could she identify with Elizabeth Taylor or Olivia de Havilland, and she had never liked Frank Sinatra in the first place.

When she finally decided to go see Jerry, the problem became one of finding a reason. It could not be admitted that she wanted to see them just because she wanted to see them. She never for an instant believed that her own personality was sufficient to engage their attention. There had to be an excuse—and the excuse was, of course, the fine thing that she had first discovered with them: the green grass that grew greener where music dwelt.

It was a Friday evening when the impulse finally came that sent her into the hurrying subway, through the rushing tunnels, and out into the piercing winds that swept through the street canyon in which was the Golden Horn. It was almost like a homecoming.

Louie, the Italian waiter recognized her immediately. "Good evening, Miss Taylor. Anyone meeting you?"

"Not tonight, Louie," as though she were an habitué. "I just thought I'd drop in and see Jerry and the boys."

"I'll get you a table right up front," Louie said. "Let me just chase those people over there. Haven't seen you or Mr. Burdette in the longest time." The dark-trousered, white-shirted figure glided through the gloom to a front table where a mildly intoxicated trio were giving a minimum of attention to the music and a maximum to the liquor.

After a moment she saw the three, two girls and a man, get up to move to another table, and then Louie came and led her up to the vacated table only a few feet from where Jerry Best's glittering trumpet was juggling a melody with skill and grace and passion. His face was intense, dedicated, rapt as it always was when he took a riff. But Don, filling in rhythm at the piano, saw her and winked. Then, when the sax took over the melody and Jerry took his trumpet down from his lips, Don reached out and touched Jerry's arm and pointed to Joyce.

Jerry saluted her with a loose, graceful gesture, pointed her out to Louie and then tapped himself on the chest, a gesture that clearly meant put everything on my bill.

Suddenly Joyce was aware that she was the focus of attention in the room. Who, she imagined them saying, is that girl up front? They made some other people move to give her a table. Who is she?

And even this mistaken flattery went to Joyce's head like wine. A homecoming. A welcome.

She felt reinstated in her own respect.

Then, as the piece ended, Jerry pulled the microphone to him, and in a voice that was half a whisper, said, "We got a special request from a charming young lady who ain't even requested it yet So the next number we're going to play is for Miss Joyce Taylor, a very special friend of ours, and it's going to be them Royal Garden Blues."

When the set ended Jerry left the stand and came directly to her table. "Come on out back with us. Ginger's out there. Louie'll hold the table for you," and she followed him through the narrow passageway that led through the kitchen and into the dressing room that was also the office of the club's owner, a man named Michell.

Ginger, in a strapless gown of gold lame pulled high to expose her shapely legs, perched on the corner of a desk. She said, "Hi, Joy! We really been missing you and Frank, kid." And the others came over in genuine pleasure.

Joyce felt her throat constricting with sentiment, and moisture gathering in her eyes.

"Ginger's making it with us, now," Jerry said. "Best damn blues-shoutin' you ever heard, and she don't weigh a pound over a hundred and ten." Ginger nodded happily. "But where the hell you been?"

"Living in town for about three months now," Joyce said.

'And you ain't even come around to see us? Man, you're flippin'!" Jerry expressed complete disavowal of such insanity. "And what ails Frank? He drop dead or something?"

"I haven't seen Frank for months," Joyce said.

"Gee, that's a drag." Then, with an agile tact, "Ginger's got a spot now, and I want you to dig her. Go on, take it Don. I'll sit with Joy at her table."

He led the way outside and they sat down. After a moment Don came out and went to the piano, feeling out a slow introduction.

They didn't give Ginger a spotlight, and she didn't need the microphone in the small room. She just came out and walked on the little space of dance floor carrying a chair. She plunked the chair down and sat down on it, not playing it for sex or anything. Then, as expressionless as, and with the folded hands of a little girl paying strict attention to a Sunday school lesson, she sang St. James Infirmary so it ripped great chunks out of your heart. She had a full contralto voice, with a low range that was almost a moan, but that could become as raw and sharp and edged as a slide trombone, and she made the words really hurt. Then she did other things—ordinary things, the kind of stuff everybody did; things like *Georgia on my Mind* and *Lover Man* and *If I Can't Sell It, Goin' Sit On It*—and each one came out like something new and strange.

Afterward, when Ginger had left the floor, Jerry asked her. "What happened between you and Frank? Something I can fix?"

"No," Joyce said. "Nothing like that. After all, he is married, and it couldn't last forever. In the long run it had to be Janice."

"She's a fine chick." Jerry said. "The greatest. I dig her."

"The funny part is," Joyce said, "I dig her, too, Jerry. But I couldn't go on seeing him and working with him every day after that. So when it happened I came to New York . . . Let me tell you the truth, Jerry. First I was going to come down here and tell you I just wanted to see you to make a contact for some charge, but that wasn't really it. I don't know anybody in New York. I'm absolutely alone here and I don't want to let anybody know where I am, but I did want to see some people I know, and have somebody to talk to and everything." She felt the tears coming.

Jerry put his arm around her shoulder, right there in front of all the people in the club, and gave her a firm squeeze. "Cool, Joy. I dig you. Listen, after we get through here we're going up town tonight. After-hours place on hundred 'n twenty-eighth. Got a session all set up. We got plenty of pot and I'll lay some on you before we cut out to keep you straight anyhow, but we'd like you to make it with us . . ."

"Hold on, man," Joyce said, suddenly smiling. "I don't dig you? What's pot?"

"That good, green Mexican grass," Jerry said. He chuckled—a sound as musical as his trumpet playing it sweet. "Going to have a jam session uptown and we'd like you came along."

"Cool," Joyce said. "The coolest."

"Solid. See you after the next set. We'll all get on a little out back."

11 ~ Transference

Things might have been all right if it hadn't been for Christmas. And they might still have been all right if, just at the beginning of December, Jerry Best's band hadn't gotten the telegram.

Joyce had fallen right in with Ginger and the boys in the band. All day long she would work like a machine tool for the *Journal,* and at night she would come downtown and have dinner in some Village spot, where it wasn't unusual for seven colored people to be seen together with a white girl, and go over to the Golden Horn, and Joy would hang around until about eleven or twelve o'clock and then go home to bed.

On Mondays, when the club was closed, she would spend the evenings with Jerry and Ginger in an apartment the dark-skinned girl had on West Twelfth Street, and somehow the marijuana would take the edge off the loneliness she felt when she saw how close Jerry and Ginger were.

The part that amazed her about them was that they seemed so glad to have her around, so willing to introduce her to their friends, so anxious to help her in anything she wanted to do.

It was more Jerry than Ginger who showed this concern for her future, because Ginger was, at bottom, an easygoing sort, given to immense indolences and occasional moods; but Jerry was a different cut—a strong, sure individual who knew where he was going, and was going there through the only channels he could find.

One evening, after they had been playing off some phonograph records on Ginger's changer, and while that talkative mood of the weed was still on them, Jerry asked, "Are you going to stick with that machine shop for keeps?"

"I don't know," Joyce said. "I hadn't thought about it."

"Well, you ought to quit," Jerry said. "That right, Gin?"

"Sure, man," Ginger said. "That place is the most uncool for you. You'll wind up so hung you'll flip. My dig is them cats up there got you working so you got no time for just plain grooving yourself."

"She means . . ." Jerry started to say.

"I know what she means, Jerry," Joyce said. "But I don't know what to do about it. It's funny with me, I never felt till just about now that I really fit in anywhere. That's something you and Gin did for me. Made me feel—right in there. I never felt it before, I goofed off in school, because I couldn't really feel I was worth anybody paying any attention to because—well, nobody in my own family felt I was worth paying attention to. You know what I mean?"

"Yes, I know," Jerry said. "Maybe I know it better than you think. You kind of get to know these things automatically when you're colored. But you can't just let yourself go, honey. You got to get in there and push. Like, I like music. Music is the greatest with me. Sometimes I dig if they took away music from me I wouldn't be nothing, but when I set off I didn't plan to be a musician. Music was like something I was going to keep for me. That was how I was going to get my kicks. But my real dig was—I was going to be a doctor.

"All the time I was in high school I worked nights as a musician. That's where I got to know Frank, when I was in high school. When we both were. Then we got out and Frank went to college and I was going to take a premedical course, see. I had the loot all saved up. I made enough gold out of music so I could pay my way. But I wanted to do it the right way. No second-rate, all-colored medical schools for me. I was after the best and I had the loot to pay my way—and I couldn't get in. Not medical school, and not even the pre-meds that I wanted.

"So one day I sat down with me and I figured it out. If you're colored there are ways to get to the top. With the breaks I could make it as a doctor—but I just didn't happen to get the breaks. And the other way was, like, entertainment. You see what colored people make the real money. They're boxers, actors, singers, writers, and musicians. One or two others break out, sometimes. But they're the freaks. Like Ralph Bunche at the U.N., and a couple of scientists and people like that. But what I had to do was—like I don't have any talent for words, and I never was specially handy with my fists—so I like stuck to the thing where I had already got a ways."

It was the first time Joyce had ever heard Jerry talk about himself. "I didn't know that," she said. "I thought you always wanted to be a musician."

"Oh. I did. But the big deal was I was going to be a doctor. Once I made up my mind though. I forgot about the other and got right in there with the blowing."

"Does all right, too," Gin said. "He's right in there with the best." She leaned over from where she sat beside him on the divan and kissed his ear.

"All right. It's cool for me. I dig it. But you got to do what you dig doing. You can't make it doing something you don't like. Way I see it, you ain't awful cool with those machine tool cats. They sound awful square."

"You wouldn't exactly call them hip." Joyce admitted wryly, thinking of Eugene Tip and his colleagues.

"So whyn't you skin an eye. Look around, honey. There's other ways of making the loot. I don't mean another kind of work. Frank said you were great for this kind of stuff; but you ought to get on like a magazine like, say, Look or something; you dig? A real magazine."

Joyce went home that night feeling that things were right. Gin and Jerry were looking out for her. You could feel safe with people like that, people who had your best interests in mind. It was the kind of thing that made you feel wanted. You could go to their house and sit down and turn on the jive, get just a little high and really feel in there. She caught herself thinking in jive, and laughed gaily to herself, making a middle-aged woman facing her in the subway give her a disapproving frown. Then she thought, maybe colored people were the real people, the right people. Maybe that was the way to live . . .

It was a hard thing for him to do, and Tony wasn't quite sure he could manage it, even when he was standing in the hallway where Estelle, the Taylor's maid-of-all-work, had left him when she went to find Priscilla Taylor. You can always make some excuse, he thought, and beat it out of here. So then he tried to think up an excuse, such as Mom sent me over to see if I could borrow a cup of sugar.

But when Priscilla Taylor came into the hallway, all Tony could think of to say was, "Miss Taylor, where's Joyce?"

The questions caught the woman completely off guard. Yet it struck her like a blow that she had always known would have to come.

Priscilla said, "Come in the other room, Tony. Leave your coat there on the seat."

He followed her into the living room. The room was immaculate and fussy. Victorian chairs confronted battery-driven electric clocks under glass domes, and annoying antimacassars and tidies cluttered the chair arms and table surfaces.

"Sit down, please," the woman said.

"Thanks, but I can't stay," Tony said. "I just wanted to know where I could reach Joyce?"

"I don't know, Tony." Suddenly she dabbed at her eyes with the handkerchief she held crumpled in one hand. "I haven't heard from her since she left."

"Well, where was she going?"

"I don't know, Tony. I don't know what to do." Her voice broke completely. "I don't know anything about that girl. How could she go away like that and not even suggest where she was going?"

"You mean she just went away like that, without even saying where she was going?"

"I've been so distraught, Tony. You can't imagine how this has upset me."

"Let me get this straight, Miss Taylor. Joy just went away and didn't say where she was going. Is that what happened?"

"Yes."

"Well what did you do about it?"

"What could I do?"

"What does Mr. Taylor say?"

"He doesn't know yet."

"You mean you haven't told them that Joy's gone?"

"I couldn't, Tony. I just couldn't. How could I write them over there in Europe that their daughter has run off? Heaven only knows where the girl has gone."

"What about the police? What do they say?"

"I didn't talk to the police."

"Look, Miss Taylor, I don't like to tell you your business, but you'd better call Mr. Taylor, wherever he is, right this minute. Did Joy leave a note or anything?"

"Yes. She left me a note. She just said that she was going away, and wouldn't be coming back. She said I wouldn't hear from her anyway, so that there was no reason for me to worry about her. That's all she said."

"You better start placing that call. It takes a long time to put a call through to Europe. Where are they now?"

"In Rome. My brother's arranging a contract there. But how can I call them? At first I thought she'd be back in a day or so. How can a young girl like that go out on her own? I knew she'd be back. And then time went by, and—and then I just couldn't. I can't."

"This happened in August, Miss Taylor. They have a missing persons bureau, the police, I mean. You call them first and then—No. I have a better idea. Let me see what I can do. I'll be back later." He went into the hallway and snatched his coat from the bench. On the porch he stood for a moment looking at the December rain and planning his movements. Then he ran across the lawn, cutting across backyards until he reached the Thrine garage. He opened the doors and backed his car out into the turn-around. For a moment he stopped there. "What if—?" But he decided there were no what-ifs, and drove on out, swinging into Central Avenue and keeping straight until he reached Randolph Road.

They had been building up to Christmas for weeks now—all three of them. All four, really, because Don Wilson, the pianist was in on this deal. The tree was purchased and mounted, and stood in the cool of the paved backyard behind the brownstone house on Twelfth Street.

It was a time of conspiracies and counter-conspiracies. Out of small sums, quietly conserved, Joyce had bought a tape recording unit for Jerry, a watch for Don, and a fine string of cultured pearls for Ginger.

She knew that Jerry had ordered a car for Ginger, because she had been with him when he had made the down-payment, and she knew that Ginger had laid out a fortune for uniformly bound Bach scores which Jerry had been studying lately.

Don had inquired of her whether she thought it would be all right if he gave Ginger lingerie and, when this scheme was rejected, had settled on a vast vase of costly perfume.

There remained only a week now till Christmas, and Joyce was working on a complex scheme of small presents to be stuffed in stockings by the useless fireplace.

With Ginger she had just returned from an expedition to secure a final miscellany of small gifts, that particular Saturday afternoon, when the doorbell rang long and loud—as though whoever were below could not wait patiently for admission, but intended to deafen them into an immediate response.

Joyce said, "Stick everything under the couch. I'll buzz downstairs." She went to the kitchen and pressed the door release. The ringing stopped, then she ran back to the hallway and, leaving the chain on, swung the door inward. Jerry came up the stairs three at a time.

He said, "Let me in, Joy." His face was hard and angry.

When she released the door-chain he brushed past her. She followed him into the living room. Ginger was still bent over, stuffing things under the couch when Joyce reached the doorway. She saw Jerry stalk across the room, stop behind Ginger, draw back his foot and kick her squarely.

Ginger toppled to the floor, then quickly twisted around to look up at Jerry.

"What's the matter with you, man?" she said.

"Got a present for you, honey. Man left this with me. Man named Roy Mallon. Roy Mallon the pusher." He tossed a small, manila-wrapped package no bigger than a ring box on the couch,

"What you talking about?" Ginger's voice was shrill and whining.

"I told you once, I want no junkies with my band. I got no time for junkies. I want nobody from my band going to any hospital, and I don't want to get hung up on no narcotics rap. Bad enough there's a law against charge. But charge ain't got no hook, and I think it's a good thing, a fine thing. But this—nobody's going to have it around me."

"Jerry!" Ginger got to her feet and came toward him.

"Get away from me. I got a few words to say. I don't know how bad hooked you are. I seen—I saw them little marks on your arms, but I couldn't believe you'd shoot it I thought they were just blackheads or pimples or something. I tried to convince myself and I let it pass. But no more. We got a wire from a Miami place, a big place. We're taking it. But you ain't coming along. I got a replacement for the band and I asked Bob Michell to let us go to Miami. It's only for two weeks, through Christmas and New Year's. He said it would be okay. So then, when I found out about you buying horse from that pusher—then I called Bob and told him you were staying. So that's all right. But when I come back if you're still on that stuff, girl, that's the end." He turned and walked out, without a word to Joyce. It was as though Joyce's whole world had exploded before her very eyes.

The dark girl stood for long seconds, just as Jerry had left her, unmoving until the slamming of the downstairs door came up through the walls. Then she ran into the bedroom and banged the door behind her. For a while Joyce could hear her sobbing. Then, after a time, the sobbing stopped.

Joyce thought, I'll wait a little longer and then I'll give her some coffee. She went to the kitchen and ran water into the pot.

Frank led Tony into the living room, trying to choke down the fear that had caught at him as he saw the boy's face framed in the doorway. When he had opened the door he had started to say, "What's the matter, Tony?" Then, hearing Janice behind him, he had laid his finger on his lips and, turning to Janice, had said, "Could you excuse us a few minutes, Jan?" And she had gone up the stairs, looking pale and terrified.

He said nothing, waiting for Tony to speak.

"I just want to know where Joy is, Mr. Burdette."

"Frank," Frank said, automatically. Then, "Don't you know?"

"Of course I don't. I wouldn't be asking if I did."

"I haven't seen her." The fright wag growing. What had happened to the kid? Had she been hurt?

"When was the last time you saw her?" Tony demanded.

"Not since the summer. What's the trouble?"

"Neither has anybody else."

"Sit down," Frank said. He dropped into a chair and extended a cigarette to the boy from a crumpled pack on the coffee table. "Let's get this straight now. I haven't seen her at all since the left the paper last summer. Sit down, fella." Tony sat down. Frank picked up the table lighter and fired both cigarettes.

"Now," he said, dragging deeply at the cigarette, "you tell me what happened and I'll tell you." Frank was getting some control of himself now.

"I had a fight with Joy just before she left. It was about you. Then, after that, we broke off. A few days later I noticed she was never around. See, I didn't really want to break off. I just thought that if I sort of blew up, well, it might bring her to her senses. Anyway, I called up a couple of times. Kind of disguised my voice so nobody would recognize it and asked for her. The maid, Estelle, said she'd gone out of town. And then, another time, she said, Miss Joyce has gone away. Nobody knows where. I let it go and let it go. But—but I couldn't get it out of my mind. I mean, Joy is very important to me. I know I'm still not of age and all that, but . . ."

Frank said, "I know what you mean." Then he said, "I think we could both do with a drink, don't you?" He said, "Where . . .?" Then he said, "Let's have the drink first." He went to the sideboard in the dining room and brought out a bottle and two glasses, placing them on the coffee table before the two chairs, and then poured out two stiff shots, all the time searching desperately for a way to begin.

Then he said, "I did have an affair with Joyce last summer. I know how that hurts you, but it's a thing we've got to get clear. And maybe I'm to blame for her going away. So we need to know that, too. What about her aunt—what's her name? Priscilla?"

"Her aunt only knows that Joy went away a few days after we had the quarrel. I don't know exactly when. She left a note that said not to try to find her. I didn't find out about it until just tonight. I thought—I thought you might know. I don't know. I thought you might have her in New York somewhere, or something."

"I don't," Frank said.

"Do you have any idea . . .?"

"Not any. Has her aunt notified—oh, but of course she has."

"No. She hasn't. That's just it. I don't know what's happened to her. I don't know, even, if she's alive. I don't know what to do."

They talked for a long time, and after a while Janice came down and talked, too.

"Mostly," Janice said, "I don't think either of you were to blame. A lot of the blame belongs to the aunt. But it's hard to blame her, really, either. The ones really to blame are Joyce's parents. Somebody's got to notify them, of course. But I don't think it will help much. The only real thing anybody can do about Joyce is wait . . ."

12 ~ Narcosis

After Joyce made the coffee, she set the pot on a tray with cups and saucers and spoons, and got some cookies from a box in the cupboard. These she arranged on a plate for maximum attractiveness. Then she laid out the cream and sugar, and carried the whole tray to the bedroom door. She listened for a moment and then tried the door. It was locked.

She knocked, gently, and then louder.

Ginger said, "Wait a second, honey." She heard Ginger getting up, heard the sound of a drawer being shut, and then the door opened. She carried in the tray, and Ginger watched her setting it down on the little night-table beside the bed.

"I thought you might like a little coffee or something." Joyce said.

She looked at the dark girl who stood there, her hand still on the knob of the door as though opening it had somehow frozen her to silence. In the light of the dim ceiling fixture Ginger's face looked strange, and there was something odd about her dark brown eyes that Joy couldn't quite place.

After a second the dark girl moved. "Gee, that's awful sweet of you, honey. That's the very sweetest. An' I hope you won't be awful mad if I don't drink the coffee right away, on account of I'm just a little upset to my stomach."

"No, Gin. Of course not. Is there anything I can get for you?"

"No, honey. Except you can sit down here with me."

That was when it really struck Joy—when she sat down on the bed beside Ginger and took the dark hand in her light one. It was as though Jerry had suddenly destroyed her home, ripping it out from under her. She thought of the things it was going to mean. No Christmas. No tree. No presents. No being together. No more evenings in the Golden Horn. No more lighting up together in the comfortable evenings, and no more going out together in the afternoons. No more feeling of safety—of being protected by the tall, handsome colored man with the small mustache; no more having a place to come home to, because it wouldn't be quite the same with just Ginger there. Her stomach seemed to be quivering with the idea, and her head ached with it

Then Ginger said, "You heard what the man said?"

Joyce nodded, holding back the tears.

"He's wrong, Joyce. This time the man is wrong."

"What do you mean?"

"What's so different about gauge and the white stuff? Nothing. You don't see him knocking off the gauge. He never put gauge down. Only reason he's so down on horse is on account of his old man."

"What do you mean?"

"What I say. His old man got on horse when Jerry was a kid. He didn't get on like a sensible guy. Not like I do. Not like other people. He used it till it was using him—till he was carrying a monkey bigger than he was."

"Who? What monkey?"

"Jerry's father. He had a bad habit. He was a real junkie. Used to get himself committed to the Government hospital for the cure, just so he could get the habit down small enough so he could afford to start all over again."

"Is that why Jerry's so down on it?"

"That's right. When he was a kid his old man used to sometimes send him out to make the contact for him. Finally they had a real hassle about it, when Jerry was in high school, and he left home."

"What's it like, Ginger?"

"It's like gauge—only a great big kick, like it takes you right through the ceiling. You get so high. You can really dig this kick." Then Joyce knew what she was going to do. She thought, I've got to find out so I'll know what to do about Ginger. And there was something else, too, that she thought. It was something fleeting, that made fleeting sense. If I know what it is, she thought, then I can tell Jerry about it and he'll come back, because we've got to get him back. Ginger and I do. She said, "Gin?"

"What's the matter, honey?"

"I want to try that stuff."

"Oh, no, honey. You don't want to get on that kick."

"Yes I do, Gin."

It went on like that, back and forth for a few minutes. Then Ginger went to the bureau drawer and took out the little packet Jerry had thrown on the couch. She opened it, unfastening the brown paper secured with scotch tape.

Inside were a series of little packets, made of waxed paper and fastened with the tape. Each measured about one-and-a-half inches square. Carefully Ginger removed the tape from the packet and spread it out flat.

"Get yourself a dollar bill," Ginger said. Joyce went to her pocket book in the other room, thinking it was funny that Ginger wanted her to pay for it. When she came back, she saw that Ginger had split the little pile of powder on the wax paper into two tiny piles. Joyce thought, where's the needle? She had seen the needle when the drawer was opened. "Give me the bill, honey," Ginger said. She took the rectangle of paper and rolled it into a tiny tube—tight, so that the opening down the center was smaller than the thickness of a toothpick.

"You do it like this," she said. She put the waxed paper with its burden of white powder on the edge of the bureau, then inserted the dollar bill tube into one nostril and bent down. Holding the other nostril, she inhaled deeply through the tube, sucking up the white powder through the tube like a vacuum cleaner tucking cigarette ash from a rug. In a moment she had disposed of the one half of the white powder. Then she rose to her feet, still inhaling at the dollar bill. When she had taken the bill from her nostril she held both nostrils for a moment, as though to keep from sneezing, batting her eyes rapidly.

"You make like that, Joy, honey," she said.

Joyce followed the same detailed procedure, holding her nostrils when she had done. The inside of her nose felt strange, a funny, cool tingling. It wasn't like tea, this stuff.

Suddenly she heard Ginger rushing from the room and saw her run to the bathroom. Then she heard the dark girl being sick—and in a moment knew why and followed her.

She vomited, strangely without effort, and then was s-o-o-o-o happy.

The pain of Jerry's going had vanished, and a million reasons why it was a good, thing came swiftly flowing into her mind. How could he not understand about this? How could he be against this? What was a "hook" compared to this? Where was marijuana when you could get like this?

Why, you could do anything, make anything, be anything. There was nothing impossible. If it were cloudy, you could make the sun shine. This was really grooving. This was being right at the top.

She followed Ginger into the living room and sat down. You could do anything, except that it was so wonderful not to do anything—just to think and feel the fine sensation of blood rushing through your veins, and hear the thoughts ticking off inside your head, and follow the thoughts as they dashed swiftly about the room, thinking things out for themselves.

After a while she said, "Ginger? Isn't the light pretty bright?" And Ginger got up, very slowly, and turned it off. Then the peace and beauty was suddenly perfect.

The great thing about it was, it was so mental. Everything was so mental, now. You could go back and relive every wonderful moment of your life, skipping all the bad parts and all the little things that had gone wrong at the time. And you could live them better than you had before, because now there was only pleasure and nothing but pleasure.

Ginger had turned on the radio, and the little dial light in the corner of the room became a friendly, protective eye. Then out came music—visible music, music that darted about the room in little blue bolts of lighting, in little colors of sound. It came so slowly, now—so much more slowly than with gauge—that every separate note had time to be counted in its individual vibrations and colors, and to develop an overlay of meanings on meanings on meanings.

Joyce let herself sink deeper into the soft armchair that felt like caressing paternal arms clasped about her body— that seemed to pick her up and carry her, like a little girl, with kisses, to bed . . .

13 ~ Tolerance

The answer to the cable that Priscilla had decided to send instead of making a telephone call—perhaps because it deferred the evil day of having to hear her brother's angry voice—came the following morning. It read:

CAN CONCLUDE BUSINESS HERE IN TWO MORE DAYS THEN WILL TAKE PLANE LANDING AT IDLEWILD THURSDAY NITE—EDWARD

She thought, you're in a great hurry about your own daughter, aren't you, Edward. But then she remembered how slowly she herself had hurried . . .

Christmas got by, somehow, and so did New Year's. Joyce spent both holidays with Ginger at the Golden Horn, where a mixed band of somewhat indifferent skill played under a white leader who served mainly to provide a background for Ginger's easy talent. Then, before Jerry came back with his anger and his storms, Ginger had a new offer from a mid-town club—a big club with a big all-colored show. And after that things began to roll faster and faster for Ginger. There were record dates and radio shows and guest appearances.

Joyce meanwhile, was learning a new language. The language of the heroin user was deeper and more occult than that of the "viper", as was determined by the relative illegality of the narcotic heroin compared to the intoxicant, marijuana. *Sniffing* and *popping* replaced *blowing* and *lighting up* or *turning on,* though the latter two might on occasion be used interchangeably with the former. Then there was *shooting it* and *mainlining it*—when you drove deep into a vein with a hypodermic needle and a solution of the white powder. There was nothing comparable to that in marijuana. But you got high on the big charge. You hit the horse, and when the stuff was real gone, you, sometimes blew your top.

You had to be careful with it. You couldn't let the habit get out of hand. A three cap habit, now, that was bad, because when you started making it with three capsules, you could get in deeper, and when it got up to six caps, suddenly, one day, you were liable to wake up all of a sudden carrying the monkey on your shoulders.

That was what they called it when it had you—when you really felt the hook. That was when you had to go out and get it, no matter what.

It didn't get like that with Joyce for a long time, and the time seemed even longer because there was so much happening in it.

After a while Ginger had shown her about the needle and taught her how to shoot the white stuff, because the other way, sniffing it, was so wasteful.

There was no money problem, because Ginger was making all the money in the world. It came rolling in, faster and faster, and you could find her voice calling to you from juke boxes, chanting at you from radios, shouting out those blues from the doorways of bars and from the windows of apartment houses, from televisions.

Then the spring began to roll in from somewhere in the Southland—but it was hard to notice the spring when there was so much happening in the little apartment on Twelfth Street.

Joyce had made some sort of peace, too, with Eugene Tip and his machine-tooled colleagues. That is, the job no longer appalled her as it had. And it was great not to be bugged just because the job was something you could do with your eyes shut.

Mr. Tip, though, was not quite as reconciled as Joyce, It seemed to be his absurd opinion that sometimes she was doing the job with her eyes shut. And it was things like that which sometimes put you to a great strain making it to work in the morning.

Things like that . . .

Jerry knew as soon as he got back. He knew when Ginger never called, never came to see him, never dropped in at the Golden Horn.

He talked about it with Don. He said, "I'm putting gauge down, Don."

"Why, man? Ain't nothing wrong with gauge."

"I know. But you got to put things down once in a while. You got to put them down so you keep being sure who's boss. Like liquor. Even cigarettes. You got to keep in the habit of being on top of things."

"No point quitting till you get beat," Don said.

"No, just running out of charge doesn't prove anything. You have to put it down when you got it. I know a couple of cats, three-four of them, that are really hooked with charge."

"But you can't get hooked."

"Not the way you can with hops or junk. Not with your body. But you can get mentally hooked, like with any kind of a crutch. You get so the way you feel happy is with grass, not with yourself. I know a cat's making maybe forty bucks a week, which is real beat loot, and he spends about twelve of it for gauge. He just lost the habit of balling without his hay. If he runs out, he can get along. But he'll go for it the first chance he gets. And it comes before most other things. Not like horse. Not before food. But it comes right after food for this cat. I don't like to owe that much to anything. Look at Ginger, man."

"Gin's doing all right. She's really grooving."

"It ain't the ball she tells herself it is. She's not really grooving. She got on that hemp crutch and walked with it so long and so hard that she got used to having a crutch stronger than her legs were. Then, when it got real hard going there, then she had to go try a bigger crutch. I know that chick, man. I got eyes for her—but not with the junk. Part that really bugs me, though, is that little chick, Joyce. She's a flipped chick. She's got a real trouble there. I only know a little about it, like her parents dumped her on her aunt, man. But nobody can make that, man.

"You got to be bugged in a way to get into any of these grooves. Big bug or little bug, you got to have a bug to turn on with anything. And Joy's got a big bug, like the kind that really throws you. And being around like that with Gin, she's digging that white stuff, and it scares me."

Don said, "You done what you could, man."

"Not everything, Don. I could of straightened her out, made things come out for her. I don't feel good with myself about that chick."

"Come on, man. Get that horn, man. Let's turn on a little jive here."

"Look, Mr. Taylor," the Chief told him, after a particularly virulent outburst of abuse, "You really can't expect a helluva lot from us. When you wait half a year to tell the police your daughter is missing, we're kind of in the position of someone who comes so late to the show he can't tell what it's all about. We've put out an eight-state missing persons alarm. The New York bureau has broadcast descriptions of the girl, but you can't count on that. Besides, she's not a criminal. She's eighteen years old now, and you can't even make her come back if she doesn't want to. Maybe she got married? You can't tell."

"Look," Taylor said, "I don't want any excuses. I don't want any stories. All I want is for you to find my daughter."

"I haven't lost any daughters, Mr. Taylor. She went—all on her own. From how I can make this thing out, you never gave a damn about her until she took off on her own. My pitch on this thing is, you and your wife got no more than was coming to you. You don't just dump a kid on relatives and let it go at that, Mr. Taylor. I'm trying to find your daughter—but I'm not doing it for you or your wife or anybody else. I'm doing it because I have to— because it's my job. The way I feel about it, she's probably a lot happier where she is . . .

14 ~ Trauma

The cops came one fine warm spring night, and snatched Ginger right out of her dressing-room at the Hot Club. It was really the pusher they were after, a man named Gonzalez, a dark little Puerto Rican with thin, hollow cheeks and great, deep-sunken eyes, but they followed him to Ginger's dressing room and they watched them make the deal through the keyhole, so they took her along too, because it was a good idea, now and then, to make an example of somebody well known—and who better than a black singer?

It happened just before Joyce got there. They had found Gonzalez with some other little packets in his pockets, and they found the stuff where Ginger had pushed it in the drawer when, they burst open the door. They found it there with the needle and the flattened-out spoon and the matches, and the little vial with a pierced rubber top that she used for loading the needle. They found everything they needed, right there in those few seconds.

And then Joyce came. She knocked at the door, and one of the cops—a federal man with no uniform—pulled it open.

She saw Ginger standing there, between two men, and there was a little dark cat, with manacles on his wrists. And then Ginger put on her act

"What the hell do you want?" she demanded

"Gin . . ."

"What right have you got to come busting into my dressing room? You, copper, get that kid out of there. You think I want everybody to know about this? Isn't it bad enough you pinch me without making a public performance of it. Get her out of here."

Then one of the cops came to the door. He was a big guy, and his voice wasn't mean at all. He just said, "G'wan. Beat it, kid. Beat it out of here."

And that was the last time Joyce saw Ginger.

Joyce woke up the next morning with the monkey . . .

Jerry did what he could. He saw Ginger, and he got her a lawyer, and he raised the bail for her with the money he had planned to spend for her Christmas car. But they were really out to make an example of her, so his offers to finance her in a private hospital didn't impress the

United States Commissioner. She waived trial and was sent to the United States Public Health Service Hospital for the full cure.

Joyce hadn't felt the hook before. But now it was in there, turning and twisting. She got out of bed, that morning, feeling there was something wrong with her. Her mouth tasted dry and fuzzy, and water wouldn't make it go away. She kept yawning; great gaping yawns that went on and on and on. Her hands trembled, and her legs were rubbery and uncertain. Her stomach kept twitching as though it were trying to detach itself from her flesh and just flatten out there inside her.

Her eyes kept watering and watering and watering, so that her vision blurred, and there was no getting them clear, and her nose felt runny, but faster and harder and looser than with a cold.

At first, not knowing what it was, she couldn't place it. She was just sick. That was the thing. The flu, maybe. But it wasn't the flu, because there was something you wanted—something you had to have. Something you couldn't wait another second for.

Then she knew what it was, and she went to the drawer where she kept the needle and the stuff. She could hardly steer her trembling fingers as she brought out the spoon with its handle bent straight so that it would hold the cup part without spilling. There were only two capsules. That wasn't going to be enough. But it would have to do for the moment. She spilled one capsule into the spoon, thought hard for a second, and then dumped in the other feeling her hands endangering the whole project.

She went to the washbowl and got out the eyedropper from the little medicine chest, and half-filled it with water from the warm tap. Then she squeezed the water from the dropper into the spoon. With shaking hands she lit a match and then picked up the spoon, holding the match under the cup and counting off the long frightful seconds until it boiled. Another match, and the boiling water dissolved the white crystals, and then it was ready. She set the spoon down and took the eyedropper and sucked it clean and dry, then she took a little pellet of cotton from the toothache kit that stood on the bureau and squeezed it into the mouth of the eye-dropper, leaving just a little tail free to pull it out with later on.

From the closet she got a belt, and doubled it through the buckle, then, slipping it over her left arm just above the elbow, jerked it tight, liking the pain because it took her mind from the great, gaping yawns that swept her again and again. She stuffed the belt under itself in a hitch so it would stay tight, then bent the arm and tightened the muscles until the veins stood out in ridges against the pale skin.

Then, because she had been too hurried, she made herself go calmly. With her cramped left arm she held the eyedropper. Then, like a laboratory technician, inserted the hollow point of the depressed hypodermic through the cotton in the tip of the dropper and into the body, then, slowly, cautiously, pulled outward on the piston.

When all the liquid had been withdrawn from the dropper, she laid it down, and took the bit of cotton from it and threw it into the washbowl in the corner. Then she held the needle, point upward, and depressed the piston, driving the fluid up into the hollow point, until just one tiny drop formed at the open point.

The swollen veins now stood out clearly. She selected a spot free of old pits, and fiercely rammed it into the vein, then slowly depressed the piston—down, down, down, all the way, then withdrew it a little, seeing the winy blood spurting up into the cylinder behind the glass piston. She allowed the blood to flush out he cylinder and then returned it to the vein with the needle Then she pulled the needle out and lay down on the bed.

In two singing seconds the yawning ceased, the shimmering tears ceased to flow in her eyes, her pulse settled to tranquility, and her stomach stopped flapping at the walls of her abdomen.

But it was not enough. There was nothing for later— nothing for the monkey. She would have to get a fix.

She knew the contacts, but now it was a question of money. Ginger had always had all the money in the world. Ginger had always paid the fix man. She looked in her pocketbook. She had only five dollars. That would get her two, maybe three caps, Not even a deck. Not enough. Not even enough for today, and what about tomorrow?

She tried to think about Ginger. Ginger in jail. Ginger going to prison. Wasn't that what they did to you? Put you in prison? But she couldn't think about her. Couldn't even take time to think about how Ginger had got her out of it—pushed her out before the police had understood what was happening. How could you think about a thing like that when this was going on, this terrible gnawing anxiety?

Joyce knew that if she had what she needed for today, five more caps, maybe, the anxiety would be gone, and she would be calm and able to function, able to do something about getting more. But now what?

Then she thought about the office and Mr. Tip. What time was it? Eight-thirty. She was due in at nine o'clock. And now Tip loomed in her mind like a great wonderful figure. The boss. The boss had to take care of his employees. That was what a boss was for.

She'd tell him—something, anything. She went out into the morning not seeing the spring sunlight, not seeing the sprouting green of the park, because all there was to think about was the terrible yearning that was coming, the great need that only money could answer.

She stood in front of Tip's desk feeling helpless and small and incompetent. He kept her standing, like that, only his bald head turned to her, and his myopic lenses closely focused on the paper that lay on the green blotter.

Joyce said, "Mr. Tip?" very tentatively.

"Yes?" He did not look up.

"I have to have some money, Mr. Tip. I don't feel well this morning and I have to go to the doctor. I wondered if I could get a small advance . . ."

He looked up at her. "Miss Taylor," he said, "your work hasn't been very satisfactory lately. I meant to tell you on Friday, but I missed you when you left. It's too bad you had to come in this morning, and I really regret the waste of your time."

"What do you mean?" It was so hard to concentrate, so hard to follow. The little nerves were tingling again, demanding, wanting, needing.

"Don't you understand?" as though there couldn't be any misunderstanding.

"No, Mr. Tip. I just wanted a small advance."

"Miss Taylor, you are discharged, as of Friday. I will be glad to supply satisfactory references if you need them." The head was down again.

All right. This was one kind of answer. She'd get the money now, anyway, and something would come up before that ran out. Two weeks salary was—ninety, less . . . "Where do I get my check?"

"What check, Miss Taylor?" The question seemed genuinely to interest him. He raised his head, and peered at her through the thick glasses.

"My two weeks."

"There is no check, Miss Taylor. We don't make a practice of paying unnecessary amounts." The head went down again. There was nothing left to do but go.

Joyce found Roy Mallon sitting, as always, on the rim of the circular fountain in the middle of Washington Square. Roy, this joyous May morning, was a happy man. He had just made a stick deal with a cat from Brooklyn, and the loot would make it a ball for him for at least a week. That gauge deal was worth a hundred to him, and he had his own comfortable stash of white stuff in his pad.

Roy tended to look down a little on the vipers—but not too much. After all, they were customers, and he did have stuff. He adjusted his sunglasses and let himself lean back against one of the gargoyle figures, feeling the charge circulating through his veins.

Vaguely he saw Joyce as she came toward him from the Fifth Avenue bus. A nice chick. Friend of Jerry's and Ginger. Too bad about Ginger. They must have been on to Gonzalez for a long time to come like that

Joyce came up and stood in front of him. She said, softly, so as not to alarm the women whose children were racing and sprawling about the empty basin of the fountain, "Look, man, I got to get a fix."

"I got a little," Roy said. "Eight a deck. Real gone. Eighteen percent."

"I can't make that," Joy said. "I'm beat. I got no loot."

"Gee, that's a drag." Roy said. "I'd fix you up, but you dig what's with my connection. It's all gold in front. I got to lay it out, and then get it back."

"Listen, Roy. I got to have that stuff. I'll get gold for you tomorrow, but I got to have a fix right now. I got to have enough to carry me the whole day and tonight."

He didn't feel sympathy. He just felt good, and this was no time to stop feeling good. You couldn't let a thing like this drag you; not when you felt so gone, so really sent. And the kid was getting hysterical. She knew where you lived. You had to do something.

"Joyce," Roy said, his sallow tanned face reflecting what sympathy it could, "I got six decks in a stash, right around here. I don't know when I'll get more. I may even have to find a fix man myself tomorrow. But I'll lay half of it on you."

"Great!" Joyce said. "The end! You saved my life, man."

"I dig," Roy said. "I'll make it back here in fifteen minutes. Now, don't cut out, now."

"I won't man. And I'll have the loot for you tomorrow . . ."

15 ~ Insecurity

That was the morning when Tony saw Joyce. He had just come out of New York University Commons, and was walking slowly across Washington Square Park toward the subway. He had left his car in Jamaica and come in on the Eighth Avenue subway that morning, and now he was un-determined whether to go back out to Jamaica and pick it up before his afternoon class began, or whether to go up to the Griddle on Eighth Street and just hang around.

Then he saw her. She was standing at the edge of the big fountain among a clutter of loungers and women air-ing their children, talking to a deeply tanned man wearing sunglasses who might have been, and probably was, a race track tout.

He saw the man hand her something which she put in her handbag. He was still on the other side of the broad thoroughfare that bisects the Square—and still not quite sure. She was more slender than he remembered her, and a little better dressed. For a moment or so he just stood there, trying to be sure before crossing the street to approach her. Then she left the tanned man and walked toward a Fifth Avenue bus. The walk was what made him sure. The even, unhurried pace, with something approaching a regal dignity.

He started to run across the street but a line of traffic halted him for a moment. When it had passed he started across again, but Joyce had disappeared and the bus had started.

She was on the bus. He knew that, and ran after it, yelling after the driver. But the bus caught the lights and was gone up past the arch before he could reach it.

He remembered the number of the bus and looked for a cab, but it took nearly two minutes, and when he had lo-cated one and followed the bus, they were unable to catch up through the heavy traffic until it had passed Forty-second Street. Then he clambered aboard the bus and looked on both decks. But Joyce was gone.

He went to see Frank Burdette that evening and told him about seeing Joyce. Frank said, "I don't see that it helps us much, except that we at least know she's alive and all right." Somehow it didn't occur to Tony to com-municate his news to the Taylors—so he didn't.

Joyce sat in the bar with a drink on the table in front of her, because she couldn't think of anything else that she wanted to do. She didn't much want the drink, but it gave her an excuse for sitting.

She was full of a sort of quiet desperation, realizing that tomorrow or the day after, whenever the two remaining decks of the white powder ran out, she was going to be through.

She had been able to get the three decks from Roy today by something that lay, in Roy's estimate, halfway between blackmail and sympathy, but that was really more the former than the latter. She knew that the pusher had said he had only the six decks of the stuff. That though, was to keep her from turning herself in to a hospital and then telling who supplied her in pique because he had refused her. Now, though, with official notice that he had no more of the stuff—even if it weren't true—she could hardly blame him for failing to supply her without payment.

And there was no chance of paying for any. She looked at her pocketbook. There was still a little more than four dollars left in her purse. She thought of Jerry Best. But he wasn't at the Golden Horn anymore. He was playing somewhere out of town, she didn't even know where. Maybe she could find out where he was—from an agent, or Down Beat or something. But Jerry was down on junkies—real down. She pictured him giving her the quick brush-off once he found out about her.

Then a man came and sat down at the table opposite her. "Hello, honey," he said. "You look lonesome."

He was young, a little over-dressed with lemon yellow tie and a dark shirt, but his face was pleasant, and having someone to talk to was suddenly vital. She had dinner with him and, at the end of the evening, took him to her room.

When she awoke in the morning he was gone, but on the dresser was a twenty-dollar bill that had not been there the night before. The money relieved all of her panic and some of her guilt. And by the end of the week her indoctrination into the profession was complete.

16 ~ Integration

The worst were the mornings because you woke up in the mornings with the feeling you had done something particularly awful the night before—though you could not quite remember it clearly. You wondered if it was the horse that made forgetfulness, or shame for your actions.

Joyce's first recollections, in that hour of the early afternoon that had become morning for her, always had to do with men, except on one or two rare occasions when there had been a woman somewhere in the evening's confusion. That had happened, too.

But, by and large, Joyce's "Johns" were little different from other men. The things they demanded from Joyce, that they could not demand from their wives or mistresses, were as much because they were paying her as because they wanted those things to happen. And the demands were more often self-imposed than coming from the men themselves. "Johns" were surprisingly undemanding—more giving, in fact, than taking!

But each demand seemed, to Joyce, only like a fresh degradation—like one more step down into the abyss into which her life teemed continually to be descending.

The problem of the "fix" seemed almost providential relief from those morning thoughts—those matutinal despairs. The remembered feeling and the taste of heroin did not come immediately when she awoke. Those first moments were dedicated to black despair. Then—next— came the thought to be seized upon, to be clung to, to be emotionally rebuilt into a problem that obliterated all other problems. The problem was: How be assured of a sufficient supply of the stuff to ward off the dire moment when you were out—beat?

You could concentrate on that, once you got around to it in your mind. You could concentrate on it while you had that special taste in your mouth, while your hands had that light sensation, while all the little nerves under your skin seemed to itch for the fine feeling of a charge. And if you kept concentrated on that one fear, all the others somehow would become pressed down—would sink out of sight. Still, with practice, the fear of being without had come to be reinforced with all the other fears until it was a ceaseless thing, and the pleasure was gone from the charge itself. The "mainline" shot was only the relief that permitted you to go in search of the next shot.

Sometimes, as this morning, Joyce looked at herself in the mirror and wondered that there were no marks or signs to indicate what went on behind the facade of flesh. She looked at her body, searching for the scars of her disintegration, and the body was firm and rounded and beautiful—as virginal as before so many hands had fondled it, molded it, compelled it into variant male-factions.

Then she went to the telephone and tried to reach Roy Mallon, looking at her watch and knowing that it was almost deliberate that she was trying at a time when he could not possibly be at home.

It felt almost as though she didn't want to reach him, as if she wanted to hear the phone ringing unanswered in that basement apartment on West 21st Street where he lived. Now and again she let herself think about that-as though she were preserving the urgency of the "fix" problem so that, all through the long evening it might press on her mind, and distract her from present reality.

When the phone had buzzed enough, and all hope had long since vanished, she dressed and made herself up. Suspants and Maidenform, Halfmoon and Arts & Ends, Bonwit's and Lord & Taylor, Chen Yu and Helena Rubenstein, Andrew Geller and Barra, John Frederics and Ohrbach's. Then a dash of perfume from Saks, a scarf from Peck & Peck, a pocketbook from Hermes. She could tell from which of her "Johns" each of them had come.

Then she went out to meet Eric.

Eric Tanger was waiting for Joyce in the bar near Madison and Fifty-third. He stood there looking exactly what he was—a man, youngish, balding, well dressed in a flashy sporting manner—a successful sharp businessman of thirty-five who some day hoped to grow out of the garment district.

Joyce said, "Hi, baby," then stepped back a little to admire him. "Very sharp," she said. "Very sharp, indeed." She flicked highly imaginary ashes from his lapels, and slipped her arm into his.

"How," Eric said, "would you like to go for a walk in the park this beautiful afternoon."

Joyce pouted. "Oh, Eric! My feet!"

"Just a stroll, my little trollop. Nothing to louse up those shapely gams. Incidentally," Eric said, "you're rather well turned out yourself this afternoon. Shall we try the Tavern on the Green?" It went like that, most of the time, with Eric. Underneath, she knew, Eric and Edsel and Marty, and John and Pelvin and Lee, were after the somewhat standardized offerings of harlotry. But on the surface they were willing to go along with her self-protective fiction that these were love affairs.

As they crossed Fifth Avenue and entered the Park they came into the full afternoon sunshine and Joyce put on sunglasses. Eric waited until they were safely in the park before he unhooked her arm from his and swung her around to face him. "Take off those glasses!" he said.

"What for?"

"Never mind, just take them off."

Reluctantly she lifted the green lenses from her eyes, blinking at the brilliant sunlight. The pupils were dilated, and seemed almost opaque.

Eric's voice was suddenly harsh. "I thought I told you I didn't want to see you when you were on that stuff."

She stood there, completely miserable, unable to say a word.

"Joy, you're no good this way. Not to me. Not to yourself. Not to anybody or anything."

She could feel the words, and the meaning of the words. But the misery was not because of the words. It was because he was dragging her—bringing her down. But the horse, singing in her blood, that could be a shield. She could let the words flow by without hurting, never really hurting, never really meaning anything, only this kind of words brought you down, down, down.

"Joy! I don't see you as just another goddamned tart. You're smart. You're on the ball. You could get out of this if you wanted to. All you have to do is try."

The words hammered against her face.

"You're not paying any attention. You're not listening. You go into this filthy dope and turn yourself off like a radio. What's the matter with you, kid?"

Joyce didn't say anything. There was nothing to say. The words had no meaning.

"Can't you see you're just going in a circle? You think I don't know what's going on with you? You think I don't see that you hate what you're doing, and you take this—this filth to hide behind while you're doing it? But can't you—haven't you enough intelligence left to see that it works the other way, too? That all you do this hustling for is to buy the rotten crap you take to hide from yourself that you're hustling? Oy! Talk about vicious circles!" Then, louder, "Joy! Do you hear me?"

"I can hear you," Joyce said. There were other things she wanted to say. But she couldn't say them because—because Eric had the money to buy her; because she had to have that money.

"Can't you turn yourself in?" he demanded. "Can't you go to a hospital and get off this stuff?"

Then whatever it was that was guarding her broke. Suddenly the utter agony of living descended upon her, and tears streamed down her cheeks. All she could say was, "Eric, leave me alone. Leave me alone. Stop it!"

Angrily then he reached in his pocket and pulled out a wallet.

He opened it and snatched out bills. "All right. That's what I'll do. Here s your goddamned money." He almost threw the bills at her. "Take it and go to hell. I don't want to see you. I don't even want to smell you—you disgusting little tramp."

And then he was walking away. It was the second time it had happened like that . . .

Frank had walked home in the pleasant May evening, disdaining the crowded bus. He heard the telephone ringing as he came up the steps of the front porch and, from upstairs, he heard Janice's voice. It said, "Oh, damn!"

He called, "I'll get it, Jan," and stepped into the hallway where be snatched up the receiver.

"Frank," the telephone said, "That you, man?"

"Jerry! Where are you?"

"I'm at the station, man. You want to drive downtown and meet me someplace?"

"Why meet you? Come on up here." Then, realizing the thoughtfulness that had prompted Jerry, he said, "Don't be a dope, Jerry. Grab a cab and get up here for dinner."

"It ain't just that," Jerry said. "I can't talk about this to front of Jan. It's about that old chick of yours, Joyce."

"Yes you can, Jerry. Do you know where she Is? How is she? Jan knows all about it."

"All right," Jerry said. "I'll make it on out there in a few minutes."

Jerry told them about it over dinner.

"I guess it was a lot my fault," he said. "But I was so damned mad at Ginger I didn't even think what it might do to Joyce, leaving her with Gin like that. Then, when Gin told me that Joyce was on the stuff, I guess I was so busy trying to swing things for Ginger that I just plain forgot about the kid."

Janice said, "The poor thing."

Jerry said, "You're really cool about this Jan. I dig that." Janice smiled, not really happily.

He went on. "After I left the Golden Horn I been working mostly out of town—so of course you haven't been seeing me around—and she hasn't been either, even if she wanted to.

"Anyway, this particular Friday night Don Wilson and I were both in on the session at the Stuyvesant Ballroom, and Joyce came up to see me. She was with a real drug cat—an ofay, the worst, the kind of guy who goes out with pros, but flips his wig when he sees the chick he's with talking to a colored cat. She didn't like this cat, much . . . Sorry, Jan. This man she was with was like a real low type. The kind of guy who goes out with—well, prostitutes, but won't . . ."

"Jerry" Jan said, "I dig you, man."

"Anyway, she said he wanted her to do things she just couldn't. I laid some gold on her. I only had fifty with me; and then I got her address. I know she doesn't dig going with men, but it seems the only way she can find the loot to buy the stuff . . .

"Jerry," Frank said, "I've got to telephone somebody. Can you excuse me a minute."

"Solid, man."

He went to the telephone in the hall and thumbed through the little book on the stand, then dialed quickly, nervously pulling the dial back round after each numeral.

"Hello. May I speak to Tony, please? . . . Thanks . . . Tony? . . . This is Frank—Frank Burdette. Get over here. Get over here quick . . . We've found her, but I don't know how long we can keep her . . . Good . . . See you." He hung up and returned to the diningroom.

After Jerry had gone, Tony and Frank talked it out.

"It wouldn't do any real good if it was me," Frank said. "It's you who must go to her. I've got to explain to you about Joyce a little. Don't get the idea that Janice would interfere with my doing it—if it would help. But the trouble is, it wouldn't. It would work quicker, it's true. But it wouldn't get her off the heroin, and it wouldn't stick. So don't think I'm ducking out of what's really my job. I'm responsible for this. But the cure lies with you, not with me. So it's got to be up to you."

"I don't get it," Tony said. "You're older than I am. You know more than I do. Why can't you do it better than me."

"Look, Tony, before I got into the newspaper racket, I wanted to be a psychoanalyst. It was the big parlor kick in those days to be a psychoanalyst, and I was all for it. I was a psych major m college, and I was set to go on with it, too. Then I got into newspapers, and I liked it and I stayed. But there are certain things you learn about people that sort of stick with you. When you establish a certain habit as a kid—oh, like Junior's getting the habit of not eating—it somehow gets built into your personality, and without knowing it, you more or less keep repeating variations of the habit all through your life. Sometimes the habit can be broken while you're still a kid. Sometimes it can be diverted, or changed into another habit when you're older. That's the kind of habit Joyce has, and we've got to break it."

"I still don't understand," Tony said. "She has a drug habit. She never had that before."

"That's right. I forgot to mention something else. Sometimes people will substitute a worse habit for another kind they've had a long time. I'll try and show you what I mean. Joy's parents began leaving her alone and dumping her off on relatives when she was very small. They kept on like that, right up till now, going off and leaving her, putting her in schools where they wouldn't have to be bothered with her. It didn't take Joyce long to get the idea that they didn't want her. It made her feel that she wasn't good enough for them to want. So she got a habit of thinking of herself as not good enough to be wanted. That's one of her habits. Do you see it?"

"Yes," Tony said, dragging the word a little.

"It shows up in several ways. She had to give people things to make sure they would want her and value her. I don't know what she gave Ruth Scott. Probably brains, because Joyce has them, and from what she told me about Ruth, Ruth doesn't. The thing with you, that first time, was typical. She gave herself to you, because she thought that sex was something you could give that would make people value you. She tried to give the same thing to the whole senior class the time she did a strip-dance in the study class. When she did it, what she was saying to herself was, 'I've got something they want. I'm valuable.' And the person she was trying to convince of this was herself."

"But why couldn't she do that in other ways," Tony said, "like other people do?"

"Well, we know a couple of reasons. Joyce managed to get her parent's attention a few times in her life. And when she did, they acted for a while as though she were valuable. She ran away from school, and when they found her they made a big fuss about her. She told me about that. Did she tell you?"

"Un-hunh," Tony said. "She did."

"That, and other, similar experiences, started another habit in Joyce. If you got in trouble, the way this other habit ran in her mind, it made people pay attention to you. So, that's what she did. She went out of her way to get in trouble."

"She did that, all right," Tony said. "She was always doing things in school to put her in hot water."

"Yes. But always with the hope of getting attention from her parents—the people who couldn't be bothered with her. I've got habits like that, too. So have you. You could probably notice mine, and I could notice yours. But neither of us can see his own. Joyce too. She isn't aware of these habits. But she has them. In psychology these would be called insecurity conflicts. But there's something else, too. Part of the urge to get into trouble is to punish her parents, because she's really angry with them for rejecting her. And that's another habit that she's carried over into her life with other people besides her parents. You were angry with her one day because she missed a date with you. So she punished you. She went out with me. And, from her habit point of view, she managed to get in trouble with me. She smoked marijuana that night for the first time. She did what her mind and emotions thought of as 'wrong things'—getting in trouble. That was because she wanted you. She has still another habit. Her parents failed to love and protect her. So she developed a habit of looking for love and protection—looking even harder than anyone else does—because we all do that. When she found love, any kind of love, she habitually tried to make a parent, a father, for herself out of the person who loved her. And the better the role fitted, the better she liked it She tried it first with you. Then, when you were angry with her, she tried me. I was older. I actually was a father. That was good. She could fit the pattern that she wanted on me more easily than on you. I was free enough of my parents—because I didn't have any around—to make a father figure for her, better than you could. Do you get all this?"

"Yeah," Tony said, a shade of surprise in his voice. "It sort of makes sense."

"Didn't you expect it to?"

"Not at first. But now it does. It was like that with Jerry and Ginger? They sort of were parents for her, too? Right?"

"That's it. Now the narcotics come into the picture. When Jerry broke up with Ginger, the shock was suddenly more than she could take. She needed something to cushion it—the way people have a drink when they're upset. For Joyce, heroin was really no different than marijuana—but it was stronger. Marijuana won't let you forget your troubles, unless they're very minor ones. But heroin will. So it was easy for her to go along with Ginger. Ginger was protecting her. Ginger was a kind of mother. She would see that nothing bad happened. But when the police took Ginger away, then she had to lean on the heroin itself. The heroin made her able to forget how desperately she needed love. The heroin let her feel good enough for herself. In a way the final step, her turning to prostitution to get the money for the heroin, was the same sort of thing. Every time a man paid her for love, he convinced her that she was worth something. Do you understand that, too?"

"Yes. I get it. But a lot of these things go on at the same time. They kind of overlap. Several habits push her at once. Is that it?"

"That's right. Now I'm one of these bad habits with her. I fit her role of a father figure too well. Jan—my wife—wouldn't object to my seeing Joy if it would save her from heroin. But I can only supply a temporary remedy. The real remedy isn't there anyway. She's a grown girl. She doesn't really want a father. She really wants a lover—a man of her own. And that's where you fit in, and I don't. Dig?"

Tony grinned. "I dig. The normal-er it is, the better. And the thing I've got to do is convince her I really love her—no matter what, but more when she's good than when she's bad."

"That's right. And it's slow. It won't happen right away. There's one other thing, too. I don't think—I'm not sure of this—but I don't think that Joyce is a full-fledged heroin addict. Not yet. Not in the physiological sense. From what Jerry could find out from one of the men who sells her heroin, she isn't taking enough for that. It hasn't been long enough for her to need that much. But if it goes on longer, then she will need it." He stood up. "If you want anything from me, any time, I'll do what's necessary."

Tony got up to go. "I'll keep in touch," he said. He was suddenly very adult.

17 ~ Resolution

She was asleep when the telephone rang. Asleep, but not undressed. Her skirt had worked up around her waist, and her blouse was open and the bra unfastened at the back. Her shoes lay on the chenille coverlet beside her feet, and she had unhooked her nylons from their panty supporter so they had fallen around her slender ankles to give them an elephantine look. The lipstick had smeared about her mouth, and made a gory display on the rumpled pillow case. Her coat lay on the floor where it had fallen when she came in, and there deep grooves from the wrinkled cloth pressed into the soft flesh of her cheeks. She had a damaged soiled look as she dragged herself up from sleep and stumbled toward the clattering instrument.

She held the open blouse together as she bent to the phone, though there was no one to see.

"Hello?" Her voice was soggy and hoarse.

"Joy? Is that you Joy?"

"Who's this?" Her head ached and there was a fierce pressure in her chest.

"Tony, Joy. It's Tony. Tony Thrine."

Her mind refused to take in the words.

"Tony! Joy. Don't you know who I am? Honeybun, what's the matter?"

She didn't answer. Her nerves crawled under her skin, and there was a fierce itching.

"Can't you hear me?"

"I hear you."

"Joy, I've got to see you."

"Look," Joy said. "I can't talk now. Call me back in an hour." She dropped the phone into its cradle and dragged her wretched body to the bureau, yanking open the drawer. Her hands shook with a fierce ague as she spilled the capsule into the bent spoon, and then were so uncontrollable that the white powder fell to the floor.

Frantically, as though her very life depended upon it, she scraped it up with a torn fragment of paper, disregarding the dust and lint that clung to the precious particles.

Then, in an easy routine that was complicated by the unmanageability of her hands, she followed the ritual formula of the junkie, slipping the needle into the scarred vein, and sucking the blood up again and again to flush out the last vital drop.

Then, with a great sigh, she sank into the worn arm-chair, letting her body relax against the shabby fabric, feeling herself come alive in one great tidal wave of relief.

After a few minutes the phone call floated, like disembodied words without meaning, into her mind. She tried to attach meanings to them, with little hooks that slipped from the letters and slid away before the whole thing could be decoded. Then, by and by, the meanings began to stick. "Tony." "Honeybun." "I've got to see you."

And with the meanings came panic. Not Tony! Never Tony! He must never see this,

She couldn't remember what she had said, she couldn't recall what she had told him. It was so ordinary to say, "I'll meet you in the bar at Fifty-second and Sixth in half and hour." Was that what she had told Tony? How did he know where she was? Had he traced her? Was he outside the front door of the house, waiting in case she came out? Had she left such an easy trail? What if he came in, now, and found her like this?

Joyce got to her feet and went over to the mirror. The fabric wrinkles had gone from her face, but the thinness had given it an artificial maturity, shearing off the round-ness of youth, molding the young skin to the bone structure.

Joyce saw nothing of that, only the wild hair, the mussed and gaping blouse, the slipped bra, the smeared cosmetics, the deep-shadowed eyes.

Got to get cut of here. Got to leave before Tony finds me. Hit the road, tart!

She pulled the blouse from her shoulders and dropped it on the floor, then reached behind her and hooked the band of the bra. She went to the washbowl and scrubbed frenziedly at her face with a damp cloth. An irritated color rose sullenly to her cheeks. Got to get out of here.

She went to the closet to look for a dress—and the phone rang again. For a long time—seven or eight rings—she stood it, and then she went and picked up the in-strument. "Hello."

"Hiya, honeybun." Tony's voice was tense, as though the enthusiasm he injected into it was costly and hard gained.

"Hello, Tony. How are you?" That was the attitude. Friendly. Cool. Polite.

"I'm fine. How is everything with you?"

The conversation was becoming more strained. Already. Joyce said, "How is everybody in Paugwasset?"

"Look, baby," Tony said. "I didn't call to talk to you about everybody back home. I want to see you. I didn't want to bust in on you, or anything. But can't we meet somewhere?"

And suddenly she wanted nothing else. It would be, almost, like—she didn't know what it would be like. But it would be wonderful. "All right, Tony. Where shall we meet?"

"Down here. In the Village?"

No. It must be, now, on neutral ground. Somewhere she had not been. Under other circumstances. She was silent, thinking.

"Or anywhere else. It doesn't matter," Tony said.

They met in a cafeteria on Lexington Avenue, where the continual tidal flow of people assured a paradoxical privacy. He was waiting for her when she came in, watched her walking across the table-littered floor, saw her looking about for him from behind dark green glasses, and finally caught her eye.

She came over and sat down at the table, letting the coat slip from her shoulders onto the chair back.

Tony knew enough about clothing to see that this was a different Joyce. She looked older in a way that he could not define. She made him seem almost kiddish.

For a moment neither of them said anything. Then Tony reached over and took her hand. "Joy, I've been trying so hard to find you—all this time."

"I didn't really want to be found," Joyce said. "How did you find out about me? Through Jerry?"

"Uh-hunh. He saw you at the Stuyvesant, wherever that is, and then he came out to see Frank, and Frank called me over and—well, here I am. I saw you once on the street. In Washington Square. You went uptown on a bus and I tried to follow you in a cab, but I lost you."

"How is Frank?" Joyce asked.

"All right." He had managed to keep that one under control, though it had plucked a chord of jealousy.

Joyce reassured him. "Don't look like that," she said. "He's a wonderful guy, but—not for me."

"What about us?"

"What do you mean, us?"

"I mean I want to see you. I want to be with you."

"Easy does it, baby," Joyce said. "You don't know about me anymore. I'm not Joyce Taylor from Paugwasset any more, I'm somebody else."

"Oh, stop it, honeybun. You just think you're different."

"Aren't people what they think they are?"

"Not if what they think is wrong."

"Look, Tony," Joyce said, "I'm not a good local talent any more. I've changed. And if you don't know about it, Jerry can tell you. Even Frank can. They know what happened. Especially Jerry. I'm bad, now. I'm different." There was a sort of a pleasure for Joyce in hearing the words coming out of her mouth—in hearing herself say these things. "You don't know what's happened to me. You don't know how I live. What I am. What I do."

"Yes, I do." He said it softly, not trying to keep the injury from showing in his face. "I know about the whole thing. About your—work. About the dope. I know all about you."

Then, because some inner feeling told him that it was the thing to do, he searched out the past in his mind and brought it up and drew it all there, in words, at the little table in the cafeteria. About Paugwasset, and boats, movies, and the Senior play in which they had appeared together. About Chester's and about Harry Reingold going to N.Y.U. with Tony. And then—more cautiously—about how Joyce's parents had come back from Europe, and how they were looking for her, and how he and Frank, with Jerry's information, had decided that whether they should be told, or not, was something for Joyce, herself to decide.

Then he said, "Honeybun, you've got to come back home. We all want you to come back. Honest."

It was as though he had pierced some kind of armor in which she had been girded. He saw she was crying and held out a handkerchief to her. She shook her head. Then she stood up. "I have to go, now," she said. "I can't stay any longer."

He didn't try to hold her. "When can I see you again?"

"I don't know. Where can I call you?"

He tried desperately to think of some place where he could be reached. But the N.Y.U. student is a transient in the Village. There is no center of communication. Frantically he searched his mind. There had to be some place, and it was clear that she didn't want him to call her. He didn't know why it was important for her that it be this way—that she call him and not he call her—but some intuition told him that it was.

Then he thought of a little craft shop on West Fourth Street. He would arrange it there, and then see them once a day. Maybe pay them something to take messages for him. He told her the name of the place, and then, because he wanted to be sure, went to a phone booth and looked up the number.

"All right," Joyce said. "I'll remember." And he watched her as she went out through the wheeling door into the hurrying avenue.

Tony saw Frank again. They sat in the livingroom of Burdette's house and drank rye with beer chasers, and Tony felt adultness coming into him as they talked—and as the soft tentacles of intoxication reached up into his mind.

"I don't know, Frank," he said. "I couldn't seem to reach her. It was like meeting somebody you haven't seen in a long time and you're still anxious to talk to them, but things have changed so much with them that everything you say has lost any kind of meaning. I couldn't even see her face, really, on account of those sunglasses."

"Sunglasses?"

"She even wore them indoors."

"She was high when you talked to her, then."

"How do you know?"

"Well, it wouldn't be surprising, anyway. The first thing that would happen when she knew she was going to meet you would be for her to get on, because she'd be afraid to face you unprotected. I imagine that for that one time, at least, it was a good thing. Because if she hadn't she would probably have run away, and hidden, and we'd never find her again."

"But what do I do?"

"Nothing."

"I've got to do something."

"Don't press her. Don't call her. Try not even to think about her. Just make sure that you get any message she does leave for you. And no matter what happens, meet her exactly when and where she tells you to. Understand?"

"Okay. I hope you know what I'm doing. I don't."

Tony waited.

Joyce went to see a doctor, somewhere in this period. She didn't expect him to be much help, and he wasn't. He recommended the substitution of ordinary sedation. Barbiturates. And gradual reduction of dosage with heroin. Even more strongly he recommended commitment to a private hospital, where all this would be seen to by medical authorities. And, as a last alternative, he suggested voluntary entrance in the U.S. Public Health Service Hospital in Lexington, Kentucky.

Joyce knew that much herself.

She tried the ex-junkies of her acquaintance. They knew more. "You got to make it cold turkey. There's no other way. You stop. You quit. The end. You can't make it otherwise. You can't cut down. You'll flip. You'll flip anyway. But you get it done."

And then there were the "Johns." She still needed the money, as she always had. Day after day, always money. Money to get straight. Money for food. Money for clothes. Always money.

She was making up her mind. You had to make up your mind. Even Roy Mallon told her, "Nothing does it, Joy, without you make up your mind. When you do, it's licked. You got to kick it—cold turkey. No tapering. No messing. Cold turkey."

But she didn't believe them. She cut it out for one day. Two days. And the third day she had to hit it again. And the next day was a postponement of stopping. And so was the next.

She wanted to call Tony. Sometimes in the morning, she lay on the sweat-damp sheets thinking of Tony, thinking how he was no farther from her than the telephone sitting there on the small table against the wall. She thought about that. And then she thought about the "Johns." Good guys, too. A little rigid. A little frightened— even of Joyce. Feeling guilty whenever they saw her, and, at the same time, wanting her, even wanting the fright and guilt of being with her. Not like Eric. With Eric it was love—of a sort—and braggadocio. He wanted to be able to talk about her. He wanted to be able to tell his friends how he had cured a bad girl of drugs, how he had made her over. He felt, somehow, that it would make for prestige. And then he would think to himself that, having done this, he had possession of her.

And that had to be avoided, too. Because of Tony.

Always Tony. And if she saw Tony again, it was the end of the "Johns." It had to be, because, even now, the thought of them and their possession of her—her ceaseless seduction of them—made the mornings harder, made the need for horse greater, made it that much harder ever to call Tony.

And then, one day, she did.

She met him in the cafeteria at N.Y.U., that second time. She was wearing sunglasses, and when she took them off her eyes looked like hard little balls, as though nothing were getting through them to her mind.

He kept telling her, "Joy, I love you. I really do. But you've got to get off this damned habit of yours."

It was all right when he didn't press. She could talk about getting off heroin, then. But if he tried to force her, tried to insist, she hardened up. That day she said, "Why should I? I'm no good to anybody. Not to anybody. I'm what they call a fallen woman. Really, that's what I am. A no good, down and out, rotten harlot." Her voice rose, and he had to take her out of the cafeteria. And then she said, "See, you're ashamed of me, aren't you?"

Tony shook his head.

She said, "Yes, you are. And you're right." Then she ran away from him, and it was another week before he saw her again.

When he did, she looked ill. Her eyes were sunken, and she seemed to have a cold. She kept yawning and sighing as he spoke to her.

He said, "Joy, you look sick. Let me take you to a doctor."

She shook her head. "No. I didn't have enough today. I—I took less. I'm trying to cut down."

He bent over and kissed her. Suddenly she was clinging to him, crying wildly. She said, "Help me, Tony. Just help me."

"I'll help," he said. "I'll always help."

That was when he knew she would make it.

But it was a long time before Joyce knew it, too. He tried to induce her to go back to Paugwasset with him, but she shook her head. "Not till I'm out of it, Tony." And the next time he saw her the sunglasses were back in place.

But the time came when she asked him to go home—to her room—with her.

The little room was stuffy and dingy and stark. Clothes were draped over the chairbacks, and the bed was a rumpled mess of blankets. He said, "Honeybun," softly, "can't you move to another place?"

Joyce said, "That's the thousandth time," smiling.

"The thousandth time I've asked you to move? No it isn't."

"Stupid! The thousandth time you've said honeybun. I'm keeping track."

They went down the ramp side by side, hand in hand, as people should who are deeply in love. It was a hot day, in mid-July, and the people on the platform, waiting for the red Long Island cars to open their doors, held coats on their arms.

Joyce said, "It feels awfully funny to know that home is so near. I always thought of it—all the time—as being somewhere way off, as far away as Europe." Tony squeezed her hand.

"Look," she said. "Well, I'll be darned. There's old Iris, up there. Dean Shay."

Tony looked. "Don't let her bother you."

"She doesn't," Joyce said, a little surprised.

"Look, honeybun," Tony said, "there's something I've got to ask you."

"What?"

"Will you marry me after I finish college?'

Joyce just nodded her head, and he kissed her. Hard. Right there on the platform.

The doors of the red train opened, and they scrambled for seats.

As the train slid through the tunnel under the East River, Tony said, "You won't be bothered about your parents any more, will you, honey?"

"I don't think so."

Then a voice from the aisle said, "Miss Taylor . . . ?" A sort of imperative question.

Joyce looked up. Dean Shay was leaning over the edge of the seat, swaying with the movement of the train. Joyce said, "Hello, Miss Shay."

The dean smiled, a little embarrassed. "I've been trying to get in touch with you for some time. It's lucky I found you like this. I just wanted to tell you that on sober second thought Mr. Mercer and I decided last fall that—well, that you needn't repeat your senior year if you wanted to go on to college. We decided that you could be allowed to take a special examination. It wouldn't be exactly fair to let things go all to pot over that one little incident."

Joyce smiled up at her. "They didn't, Miss Shay. I just thought they did."

THE END

A GLOSSARY OF JIVE

Jive-talk is both a code-speech for the protection of its users, and a sort of spoken shorthand for a group of people whom psychologists would call "non-verbal." The adoption of "jive" as a criminal argot by the narcotics community is, in reality, the piracy of an established speech form for use as a verbal concealment code.

"Jive," in this use, was taken over from musicians who developed it to simplify their verbal problems. For the musician, this simplified speech makes possible, in a total vocabulary of only a few hundred words, a delicate pattern of facile communication in which only approximate word meanings are required.

Thus each "jive" word carries a vast load of multiple meanings. The particular value of a word, in any given sentence, is entirely dependent on the context.

Typical of the whole patois is the word "jive." In its original usage, "jive" meant a particular type of hot music. But it has come by evolution to mean: Marijuana, nonsense ("Don't give me any of that jive!"), sex, joy, heroin, and also lends a name to the jargon itself. As a verb it means: to dance, to smoke marijuana, to be happy, to distort facts, to make music, to get high, etc. etc.

The vocabulary given here is incomplete, and applies only to the jargon as it is used in this book.

N. R. DE MEXICO

ball—to have a good time, to enjoy; as "to have a ball".
beat—out of supply (of money or drugs).
beat for—lacking.
beat loot—poor pay, small money.
best, the—very nice, pleasant
big deal—the main transaction or thing; also, a large purchase of drugs or marijuana.
blow—to play an instrument (any instrument).
bug—to make crazy, to drive insane.
bugged—emotionally disturbed.

cap—capsule (of heroin).

carry a monkey—to be addicted; to require a heavy dosage of a narcotic.

cat—person, particularly a person who knows music or frequents musical circles.

charge—marijuana (in general); also, a single shot of heroin.

charged—high on marijuana or narcotics.

chick—girl; woman.

clean—with no supply (of marijuana or narcotics).

cold turkey—to be abruptly and permanently deprived of drugs; as "a cold turkey cure".

connection—a person with a source of supply (of drugs).

contact—a source of supply (of drugs).

cool—relaxed, happy, safe, comfortable, good, pleasant.

cure—usually, gradual or progressive deprivation of a narcotic.

cut on out—leave, depart.

cut out—to leave.

deck—a measured quantity of narcotic.

dig—to understand, see, follow (as a conversation), like, enjoy; also, attitude; also, line of business.

drag—a discomfort; an unpleasantness; to make uncomfortable or unpleasant; to be an unpleasant person.

drug cat—an unpleasant person.

end, the—wonderful! terrific!

fall in—fit in with the group.

fall out—to leave.

five, give me—shake hands (five fingers).

fix-man—a narcotics pusher.

fix—a supply of narcotics.

flip—to lose emotional control; a disturbed person.

flipped—emotionally disturbed; more rarely, insane.

flip your wig—go crazy.

gauge—marijuana.

get off—to quit the use of drugs.

get on—to get high.

get straight—secure a supply of marijuana, narcotics or money.

gold—money.

gold in front—payment in advance.

gone—powerful, as "This is real gone gauge." Also, happy.

goofball—narcotic pill; also, an unbalanced person.

goof off—blunder.

grass—marijuana.

great—nice; okay.

greatest—very nice; pretty good.

groove—to enjoy oneself; also, solid, legitimate, as "He's in the groove." Also, spirit, mood or style, as "that Dixieland groove".

habit—addiction; also, degree of addiction, as "a three-cap habit, a five-cap habit.

hard stuff—any of the narcotic drugs, as distinguished from marijuana.

hassle—fight, argument

have eyes—to want, desire, as "I got eyes for that chick." Also, to be in love with.

hay—marijuana.

hemp—marijuana.

high—intoxicated.

high on lush—intoxicated on liquor rather than drugs.

hip—in the know.

hook—in a narcotics addict, the physiological requirement which compels him to return again and again to the drug.

horse—heroin.

hot—passionate, as to "play (music) hot"; compare Italian classical music terminology, *con fuoco* . . . i.e, with fire.

hung up—in a state of depression; unable to function.

hustler—harlot

in the groove—exactly right (from the fitting of a needle into a phonograph record track.

in there—participating; meeting social or musical demands.

jam—to improvise.

jam session—see: session.

jive—music, marijuana, etc., etc.

john—client of a hustler.

joy-pop—injection of heroin beneath skin (rather than into vein).

junky—heroin addict.

kick—the emotional state accompanying being high; any strongly pleasurable emotional state.

kick a habit—to break a habit: specifically, the drug habit.

lay on—to give some of, as "I'm going to lay a stick on you."

light up—get high.

lift—sensation or state of being high.

loot—money.

mainline—injection of heroin into a vein.

make it—to achieve a goal; to get along (in a given situation).

Mexican grass—imported marijuana.

narcotics rap—jail sentence for possession of narcotics.

O—an ounce of marijuana.

ofay—Negro word for unliked white people.

on—high; also, addicted.

O-Z—an ounce of marijuana.

pad—home or apartment.

pot—marijuana.

pro—hustler.

pusher—drug or marijuana seller.

put down—to reject; refuse.

riff—solo musical passage, often improvised.

set—group of musical numbers played by orchestra between rests.

sent—made happy.

session—group gathering of musicians to play, particularly to improvise.

sharp—fashionable in a flashy manner; also shrewd, clever.

shoot—inject (heroin) with hypodermic needle.

shoot it—inject heroin with hypodermic needle.

skin-pop—same as joy-pop; also, accidentally missing vein while injecting heroin.

sniff—to take heroin by inhalation through nostril.

solid—Understood! (As it were, "the connection between us is solid.")

square—bourgeois, conventional, provincial, stupid, ill-informed, not hip.

stash—concealed supply of drugs; to conceal.

stick—marijuana cigarette.

stick deal—sale of pre-manufactured marijuana cigarettes, as distinguished from sale of marijuana in bulk.

straight—supplied; stocked up.

stuff—marijuana, heroin, cocaine.

through the ceiling—very high.

turn off—to become sober; to come down from a "high".

turn on—to smoke marijuana; to take narcotics.

uncool—dangerous, unpleasant, uncomfortable, unsatisfactory.

weed—marijuana.

white stuff—heroin; cocaine.

RAMBLE HOUSE's

HARRY STEPHEN KEELER WEBWORK MYSTERIES

(RH) indicates the title is available ONLY in the RAMBLE HOUSE edition

The Ace of Spades Murder
The Affair of the Bottled Deuce (RH)
The Amazing Web
The Barking Clock
Behind That Mask
The Book with the Orange Leaves
The Bottle with the Green Wax Seal
The Box from Japan
The Case of the Canny Killer
The Case of the Crazy Corpse (RH)
The Case of the Flying Hands (RH)
The Case of the Ivory Arrow
The Case of the Jeweled Ragpicker
The Case of the Lavender Gripsack
The Case of the Mysterious Moll
The Case of the 16 Beans
The Case of the Transparent Nude (RH)
The Case of the Transposed Legs
The Case of the Two-Headed Idiot (RH)
The Case of the Two Strange Ladies
The Circus Stealers (RH)
Cleopatra's Tears
A Copy of Beowulf (RH)
The Crimson Cube (RH)
The Face of the Man From Saturn
Find the Clock
The Five Silver Buddhas
The 4th King
The Gallows Waits, My Lord! (RH)
The Green Jade Hand
Finger! Finger!
Hangman's Nights (RH)
I, Chameleon (RH)
I Killed Lincoln at 10:13! (RH)
The Iron Ring
The Man Who Changed His Skin (RH)
The Man with the Crimson Box
The Man with the Magic Eardrums
The Man with the Wooden Spectacles
The Marceau Case
The Matilda Hunter Murder
The Monocled Monster

The Murder of London Lew
The Murdered Mathematician
The Mysterious Card (RH)
The Mysterious Ivory Ball of Wong Shing Li (RH)
The Mystery of the Fiddling Cracksman
The Peacock Fan
The Photo of Lady X (RH)
The Portrait of Jirjohn Cobb
Report on Vanessa Hewstone (RH)
Riddle of the Travelling Skull
Riddle of the Wooden Parrakeet (RH)
The Scarlet Mummy (RH)
The Search for X-Y-Z
The Sharkskin Book
Sing Sing Nights
The Six From Nowhere (RH)
The Skull of the Waltzing Clown
The Spectacles of Mr. Cagliostro
Stand By—London Calling!
The Steeltown Strangler
The Stolen Gravestone (RH)
Strange Journey (RH)
The Strange Will
The Straw Hat Murders (RH)
The Street of 1000 Eyes (RH)
Thieves' Nights
Three Novellos (RH)
The Tiger Snake
The Trap (RH)
Vagabond Nights (Defrauded Yeggman)
Vagabond Nights 2 (10 Hours)
The Vanishing Gold Truck
The Voice of the Seven Sparrows
The Washington Square Enigma
When Thief Meets Thief
The White Circle (RH)
The Wonderful Scheme of Mr. Christopher Thorne
X. Jones—of Scotland Yard
Y. Cheung, Business Detective

Keeler Related Works

A To Izzard: A Harry Stephen Keeler Companion by Fender Tucker — Articles and stories about Harry, by Harry, and in his style. Included is a compleat bibliography.

Wild About Harry: Reviews of Keeler Novels — Edited by Richard Polt & Fender Tucker — 22 reviews of works by Harry Stephen Keeler from *Keeler News*. A perfect introduction to the author.

The Keeler Keyhole Collection: Annotated newsletter rants from Harry Stephen Keeler, edited by Francis M. Nevins. Over 400 pages of incredibly personal Keeleriana.

Fakealoo — Pastiches of the style of Harry Stephen Keeler by selected demented members of the HSK Society. Updated every year with the new winner.

RAMBLE HOUSE's OTHER LOONS

Mysterious Martin, the Master of Murder — Two versions of a strange 1912 novel by Tod Robbins about a man who writes books that can kill.

The Master of Mysteries — 1912 novel of supernatural sleuthing by Gelett Burgess

Dago Red — 22 tales of dark suspense by Bill Pronzini

The Night Remembers — A 1991 Jack Walsh mystery from Ed Gorman.

Four Gelett Burgess Novels — *The Master of Mysteries, The White Cat, Two O'Clock Courage, Ladies in Boxes,* with more to come from Surinam Turtle Press

The Organ Reader — A huge compilation of just about everything published in the 1971-1972 radical bay-area newspaper, *THE ORGAN.*

Old Times' Sake — Short stories by James Reasoner from Mike Shayne Magazine

Freaks and Fantasies — Eerie tales by Tod Robbins, collaborator of Tod Browning on the film FREAKS.

Four Jim Harmon Sleaze Double Novels — *Vixen Hollow/Celluloid Scandal, The Man Who Made Maniacs/Silent Siren, Ape Rape/Wanton Witch* and *Sex Burns Like Fire/Twist Session.* More doubles to come!

Marblehead: A Novel of H.P. Lovecraft — A long-lost masterpiece from Richard A. Lupoff. Published for the first time!

The Compleat Ova Hamlet — Parodies of SF authors by Richard A. Lupoff – New edition!

The Secret Adventures of Sherlock Holmes — Three Sherlockian pastiches by the Brooklyn author/publisher, Gary Lovisi.

The Universal Holmes — Richard A. Lupoff's 2007 collection of five Holmesian pastiches and a recipe for giant rat stew.

Four Joel Townsley Rogers Novels — By the author of *The Red Right Hand: Once In a Red Moon, Lady With the Dice, The Stopped Clock, Never Leave My Bed*

Two Joel Townsley Rogers Story Collections — Night of Horror and Killing Time

Twenty Norman Berrow Novels — *The Bishop's Sword, Ghost House, Don't Go Out After Dark, Claws of the Cougar, The Smokers of Hashish, The Secret Dancer, Don't Jump Mr. Boland!, The Footprints of Satan, Fingers for Ransom, The Three Tiers of Fantasy, The Spaniard's Thumb, The Eleventh Plague, Words Have Wings, One Thrilling Night, The Lady's in Danger, It Howls at Night, The Terror in the Fog, Oil Under the Window, Murder in the Melody, The Singing Room*

The N. R. De Mexico Novels — Robert Bragg presents *Marijuana Girl, Madman on a Drum, Private Chauffeur* in one volume.

Four Chelsea Quinn Yarbro Novels featuring Charlie Moon — *Ogilvie, Tallant and Moon, Music When the Sweet Voice Dies, Poisonous Fruit* and *Dead Mice*

The Green Toad — Impossible mysteries by Walter S. Masterman – More to come!

Two Hake Talbot Novels — *Rim of the Pit, The Hangman's Handyman.* Classic locked room mysteries.

Two Alexander Laing Novels — *The Motives of Nicholas Holtz* and *Dr. Scarlett,* stories of medical mayhem and intrigue from the 30s.

Four David Hume Novels — Corpses Never Argue, Cemetery First Stop, Make Way for the Mourners, Eternity Here I Come, *and more to come.*

Three Wade Wright Novels — *Echo of Fear, Death At Nostalgia Street* and *It Leads to Murder,* with more to come!

Four Rupert Penny Novels — *Policeman's Holiday, Policeman's Evidence, Lucky Policeman* and *Sealed Room Murder,* classic impossible mysteries.

Five Jack Mann Novels — Strange murder in the English countryside. *Gees' First Case, Nightmare Farm, Grey Shapes, The Ninth Life, The Glass Too Many.*

Six Max Afford Novels — *Owl of Darkness, Death's Mannikins, Blood on His Hands, The Dead Are Blind, The Sheep and the Wolves* and *Sinners in Paradise* by One of Australia's finest novelists.

Five Joseph Shallit Novels — *The Case of the Billion Dollar Body, Lady Don't Die on My Doorstep, Kiss the Killer, Yell Bloody Murder, Take Your Last Look.* One of America's best 50's authors.

Two Crimson Clown Novels — By Johnston McCulley, author of the Zorro novels, *The Crimson Clown* and *The Crimson Clown Again.*

The Best of 10-Story Book — edited by Chris Mikul, over 35 stories from the literary magazine Harry Stephen Keeler edited.

A Young Man's Heart — A forgotten early classic by Cornell Woolrich

The Anthony Boucher Chronicles — edited by Francis M. Nevins
Book reviews by Anthony Boucher written for the *San Francisco Chronicle,* 1942 –
1947. Essential and fascinating reading.
Muddled Mind: Complete Works of Ed Wood, Jr. — David Hayes and Hayden Davis
deconstruct the life and works of a mad genius.
Gadsby — A lipogram (a novel without the letter E). Ernest Vincent Wright's last work,
published in 1939 right before his death.
My First Time: The One Experience You Never Forget — Michael Birchwood — 64 true
first-person narratives of how they lost it.
The Black Box — Stylish 1908 classic by M. P. Shiel. Very hard to find.
The Incredible Adventures of Rowland Hern — Rousing 1928 impossible crimes by
Nicholas Olde.
Slammer Days — Two full-length prison memoirs: *Men into Beasts* (1952) by George
Sylvester Viereck and *Home Away From Home* (1962) by Jack Woodford
Beat Books #1 — Two beatnik classics, *A Sea of Thighs* by Ray Kainen and *Village
Hipster* by J.X. Williams
Ruled By Radio — 1925 futuristic novel by Robert L. Hadfield & Frank E. Farncombe
Murder in Silk — A 1937 Yellow Peril novel of the silk trade by Ralph Trevor
The Case of the Withered Hand — 1936 potboiler by John G. Brandon
Inclination to Murder — 1966 thriller by New Zealand's Harriet Hunter
Invaders from the Dark — Classic werewolf tale from Greye La Spina
Fatal Accident — Murder by automobile, a 1936 mystery by Cecil M. Wills
The Devil Drives — A prison and lost treasure novel by Virgil Markham
Dr. Odin — Douglas Newton's 1933 potboiler comes back to life.
The Chinese Jar Mystery — Murder in the manor by John Stephen Strange, 1934
The Julius Caesar Murder Case — A classic 1935 re-telling of the assassination by
Wallace Irwin that's much more fun than the Shakespeare version
West Texas War and Other Western Stories — by Gary Lovisi
The Contested Earth and Other SF Stories — A never-before published space opera
and seven short stories by Jim Harmon.
Tales of the Macabre and Ordinary — Modern twisted horror by Chris Mikul, author of
the *Bizarrism* series.
The Gold Star Line — Seaboard adventure from L.T. Reade and Robert Eustace.
The Werewolf vs the Vampire Woman — Hard to believe ultraviolence by either
Arthur M. Scarm or Arthur M. Scram.
Black Hogan Strikes Again — Australia's Peter Renwick pens a tale of the outback.
Don Diablo: Book of a Lost Film — Two-volume treatment of a western by Paul Lan-
dres, with diagrams. Intro by Francis M. Nevins.
The Charlie Chaplin Murder Mystery — Movie hijinks by Wes D. Gehring
The Koky Comics — A collection of all of the 1978-1981 Sunday and daily comic strips
by Richard O'Brien and Mort Gerberg, in two volumes.
Suzy — Another collection of comic strips from Richard O'Brien and Bob Vojtko
Dime Novels: Ramble House's 10-Cent Books — *Knife in the Dark* by Robert Leslie
Bellem, *Hot Lead* and *Song of Death* by Ed Earl Repp, *A Hashish House in New York*
by H.H. Kane, and five more.
Blood in a Snap — The *Finnegan's Wake* of the 21st century, by Jim Weiler and Al Go-
rithm
Stakeout on Millennium Drive — Award-winning Indianapolis Noir — Ian Woollen.
Dope Tales #1 — Two dope-riddled classics; *Dope Runners* by Gerald Grantham and
Death Takes the Joystick by Phillip Condé.
Dope Tales #2 — Two more narco-classics; *The Invisible Hand* by Rex Dark and *The
Smokers of Hashish* by Norman Berrow.
Dope Tales #3 — Two enchanting novels of opium by the master, Sax Rohmer. *Dope*
and *The Yellow Claw.*
Tenebrae — Ernest G. Henham's 1898 horror tale brought back.
The Singular Problem of the Stygian House-Boat — Two classic tales by John Ken-
drick Bangs about the denizens of Hades.
Tiresias — Psychotic modern horror novel by Jonathan M. Sweet.
The One After Snelling — Kickass modern noir from Richard O'Brien.
The Sign of the Scorpion — 1935 Edmund Snell tale of oriental evil.
The House of the Vampire — 1907 poetic thriller by George S. Viereck.
An Angel in the Street — Modern hardboiled noir by Peter Genovese.
The Devil's Mistress — Scottish gothic tale by J. W. Brodie-Innes.
The Lord of Terror — 1925 mystery with master-criminal, Fantômas.
The Lady of the Terraces — 1925 adventure by E. Charles Vivian.
My Deadly Angel — 1955 Cold War drama by John Chelton
Prose Bowl — Futuristic satire — Bill Pronzini & Barry N. Malzberg .

Satan's Den Exposed — True crime in Truth or Consequences New Mexico — Award-winning journalism by the *Desert Journal*.

The Amorous Intrigues & Adventures of Aaron Burr — by Anonymous — Hot historical action.

I Stole $16,000,000 — A true story by cracksman Herbert E. Wilson.

The Black Dark Murders — Vintage 50s college murder yarn by Milt Ozaki, writing as Robert O. Saber.

Sex Slave — Potboiler of lust in the days of Cleopatra — Dion Leclerq.

You'll Die Laughing — Bruce Elliott's 1945 novel of murder at a practical joker's English countryside manor.

The Private Journal & Diary of John H. Surratt — The memoirs of the man who conspired to assassinate President Lincoln.

Dead Man Talks Too Much — Hollywood boozer by Weed Dickenson

Red Light — History of legal prostitution in Shreveport Louisiana by Eric Brock. Includes wonderful photos of the houses and the ladies.

A Snark Selection — Lewis Carroll's *The Hunting of the Snark* with two Snarkian chapters by Harry Stephen Keeler — Illustrated by Gavin L. O'Keefe.

Ripped from the Headlines! — The Jack the Ripper story as told in the newspaper articles in the *New York* and *London Times*.

Geronimo — S. M. Barrett's 1905 autobiography of a noble American.

The White Peril in the Far East — Sidney Lewis Gulick's 1905 indictment of the West and assurance that Japan would never attack the U.S.

The Compleat Calhoon — All of Fender Tucker's works: Includes *The Totah Trilogy*, *Weed, Women and Song* and *Tales from the Tower,* plus a CD of all of his songs.

RAMBLE HOUSE

Fender Tucker, Prop.
www.ramblehouse.com   fender@ramblehouse.com
318-455-6847   443 Gladstone Blvd. Shreveport LA 71104